The Mysterious Tunnel

D.L. Ford

Matt. 6:8

D.L. Ford

ISBN: 1548368334
ISBN-13: 978-1548368333

DEDICATION

This book is dedicated to the memory of my dad,
Harold Glenn "Pete" Ford.
He was not only a good father and a good man, he was
also the greatest supporter of my writing and my best book
salesman. I miss you, dad. Till we meet again.

CONTENTS

ACKNOWLEDGMENTS

This novel is a work of fiction. Although some of the locales are based on actual locations, the characters, incidents, and dialogues are products of the author's imagination and are not to be construed as real. Any resemblance to actual persons, living or dead, is entirely coincidental. To those fellow writers who have added support and inspiration to this project, I say "Huzzah!"

1 A SICK FRIEND

The rain was misting on his windshield as Joshua Carson drove towards Pine Ridge, the town on the other side of the mountain from Brooksville where he lived. His mind was so preoccupied that he didn't even notice the rain on the windshield until there was so much of it that he couldn't see the road well enough to drive. The night before, his friend from church camp, Rachel Lynn Ferguson, had called and asked him to come over and help her pray for her neighbor. He felt the phone call was a little odd, since their friendship for the most part consisted of two weeks of church camp each summer and occasional emails through the rest of the year. Although the two towns weren't far apart, the mountain in between kept most people from going back and forth much. Most folks just found it more convenient to not take the extra effort to cross over and would travel in the opposite direction. This puzzled him all the more when he tried to figure out why she had called him. Surely there was someone over on that side of the mountain who could pray just as well as he could. Why had she called him to join her and not her own pastor? That question was still fresh in his mind as he pulled into the parking lot of the convenience store they had agreed to meet at. It appeared it wouldn't take long to ask his question because he could see Rachel Lynn standing outside the store waiting for him. He could see she recognized him as he pulled into a parking space close to where she was standing. She practically ran to his door as the car came to a stop. She was already talking to him before he even got out of the car, so he immediately knew she thought the reason for calling him was pretty important.

"Oh, Joshie, I'm so glad you came!"

"You know I never liked you calling me that," he responded with a laugh.

"Yeah, and you know I always call you that because you don't like me calling you that."

"Well, maybe someday you'll forget and just call me Joshua like everyone else," he said, still laughing. "So tell me what's going on. Tell me what's so important that you wanted me to come over here for this. Something about praying for someone wasn't it?"

"It's my neighbor, Sarah. She's very sick. None of the doctors seem to know what to do. They say it's some rare disease they've never seen before. Nothing they try seems to do anything, unless it makes her worse."

"I see. But what do you need me for? You know how to pray. I'm sure your pastor would join you in prayer too."

"I have prayed for her, Joshie. So has my pastor. We've all prayed for her and still nothing changes. It's as if God isn't listening to us."

"God has his own way of doing things. His own timetable. Just because we say a prayer, doesn't mean it will immediately happen. That would be our will being done, and we're not God. You know all that, I'm not telling you anything you don't already know."

"Yeah, I know. But I heard through the grapevine about how you guys had some pretty powerful miracles happening over there where you're at. I heard you were a big part of it."

"I witnessed God doing some powerful things up close. I was there, he did some work though me, but I didn't really do anything myself. I'm sure you're just as willing to let God work through you. You didn't need me."

"You're too modest, Joshie. I can feel the air in the room change when you're around. You're special."

Joshua just hung his head, not wanting that kind of attention and not knowing what to say.

"You are, Joshie. You're special and we need that here. Right now."

Joshua just shook his head before he looked her in the eye.

"Okay, one more time. That's God you're feeling. He is special, not me. I just let him do his thing through me as best I can. I can understand you wanting your friend to be healed, but if that's going to happen, it will be God doing it, not me."

"There's a little more to it than that, Joshua."

The sudden change from "Joshie" to "Joshua" caught his attention immediately.

"Oh? Tell me about it."

"My neighbor, Sarah, is saved. She's a really sweet girl that loves the Lord. She wants to be healed, but accepts the worst thing that will happen is that she'll be with Jesus and she's fine with that."

"And the 'more' to this story is?"

"It's her sister. She's the exact opposite. A sort of wild child, if you will. She already has a pretty bad reputation at school. Their mother is so afraid that if Sarah dies, her sister will go off the deep end and she'll end up losing both of her daughters."

"And you've tried talking to the sister?"

"We've all tried, Joshua. Instead of listening, she's built a big wall around herself that we can't get through. No matter how hard we try, it just seems like we make things worse. I'm frustrated, her mother is frustrated, even our pastor has given up on her and has given it over to the Lord. You're my last hope, Joshua. I'm hoping it will be sort of like how when kids will listen to anyone but their own parents even if the advice they give them is the same. I was hoping the difference of your voice and being a stranger just might get through to her."

Joshua got quiet and began to go over in his mind everything Rachel Lynn had told him. He knew the only thing that made him different from anyone else was the power of the Holy Spirit within him, not anything of himself. He had no problem praying for someone else, but he was afraid if any sort of healing occurred that he would get all the credit and he knew he would deserve none of it. This was really starting to trouble him. Then there was the whole matter of the "wild child" sister. He almost felt like the very soul of this girl he hadn't even met yet hung in the balance over what his actions would be.

"Rachel Lynn, do you mind if I sit in my car and pray about this a bit? It's pretty heavy stuff."

"I'd expect nothing less from you Joshie." replied Rachel Lynn sweetly, appearing very relieved he was seriously considering the situation.

Joshua knew even before his car door closed that he would help. Even though he was hesitant in his conversation with Rachel Lynn, he knew that he was guided by the Spirit to make this trip. He knew when he hesitated, it was his own self being hesitant, not being in tune with God's will. He knew that if there were any way this situation would work out for the good, it would have to be God's doing, not his.

"Lord, let your will be done," he prayed silently to himself. He didn't know what to ask for, what they would face in this battle for a soul. Deep within his being, he knew this battle had little to do with the healing of the other girl. He had felt the pull of the Holy Spirit the whole way here, but he didn't know why. It would be great if the girl was healed, but he had a strong feeling now this whole trip wasn't about her, it was about saving her sister. He knew that God would guide his steps in this battle, just as he'd been guided in the past. He just didn't know how. He opened his eyes and saw Rachel Lynn standing there beside his car looking at him patiently.

"Well?" she asked as Joshua got out of the car. "Are you in? Will you do it?"

Joshua looked at her standing there with a look of desperation in her eyes. "Yes. Yes, I'm in. I'm not sure where any of this will lead, but I'm pretty sure this is where God wants me to be. Where are these girls at?"

"That's my car over there," said Rachel Lynn as she pointed to a small, greenish sedan in the corner of the parking lot. "Follow me, and I'll lead you over to their house."

It was only a short drive from the store to their destination. Pine Ridge was a small town, much like Joshua's hometown of Brooksville. The houses were old, but the section of town they were in was a good section of town and all the homes were well kept, the lawns carefully manicured. The house Rachel Lynn was stopping in front of was equally well kept, although the lawn looked a little worse for wear, obviously neglected due to the demands of an ill child. From a distance, he also noticed a small group of people at the front of the house by the steps to the front porch. As he got closer, he noticed they all appeared to be close to his age. All of them were dressed in dark clothes adorned with chains and spikes and holes that were obviously added by design and not from wear. Some of them had multi-colored hair, others looked like they had never washed their hair. Joshua learned long ago not to judge people by their appearance, but there was something about them, perhaps their body language, that made the hair on the back of his neck stand up. He felt like a rabbit walking past a pack of hungry coyotes as Rachel Lynn led him up the steps to the front door. His smile and nod to them as he and Rachel Lynn walked up the steps being ignored didn't help that feeling a bit either. He always tried to give people the benefit of the doubt with regards to their integrity, yet he still felt it was necessary to keep an eye on them as Rachel Lynn knocked on the front door.

Rachel Lynn only had to knock on the door a few times before it opened up slowly. Joshua couldn't help but notice how tired the lady who answered the door looked. Obviously having two daughters in distress was taking a toll on her. Even with all the burdens that were weighing on her, the smile on the lady's face as she opened the door seemed genuine, not forced.

"Hello Rachel Lynn, it's so good to see you again. I see you brought a friend with you too. Won't you both come in?"

"Thank you, Mrs. Friede. This is my friend, Joshua. Joshua, this is my friend Sarah's mother."

"Pleased to meet you ma'am."

"Well, aren't you the polite one? It's always nice to meet a fine young man like you. I don't often get that pleasure."

Joshua couldn't help but think to himself what she had just said was in reference to the guys hanging around out front.

"Won't you both come in? I'm sure Sarah will be more than happy to see you both. We haven't been getting many visitors lately. In fact, it's been awhile since anyone besides you has been here to see her, Rachel Lynn."

"That's just everyone else's loss, Mrs. Friede. It's always a pleasure for me to spend time with Sarah."

"Oh, you're too kind, Rachel Lynn. You've always been kind." Mrs. Friede had to turn her head to hide the tears that were welling up in her eyes.

"You're the one that's always been too kind, Mrs. Friede. And speaking of kind, wait till you get to know my friend, Joshie, better."

He winced a bit when the dreaded name "Joshie" came from her lips again, but tried to hide it.

"Well if you think so highly of Joshua, I'm sure Sarah will too." Mrs. Friede had noticed Joshua wincing at Rachel Lynn's nickname for him and the humor of it had brought her momentarily out of her moment of sadness.

"Oh, I have a feeling Sarah will really like him. I brought Joshie along especially so we could all pray together."

Again with the "Joshie." Mrs. Friede also noticed Joshua's annoyed look and chuckled to herself silently.

"You two are just wasting your time here with me. Just go on in to Sarah's room. You know the way, Rachel Lynn."

"Thanks Mrs. F. C'mon Joshie!"

Joshua just sighed at the use of the dreaded nickname and followed Rachel Lynn as she led him up the stairs. As he climbed the steps behind Rachel Lynn, he noticed more than a few pictures of Sarah holding ribbons and awards along with a few plaques on the wall with her name for different awards and honors.

"Odd," he thought to himself. "There's no sign of the sister here, almost like this is a one child home."

He tucked that thought away in the back of his mind as Rachel Lynn knocked on the door to Sarah's room.

"Are you awake Sarah? It's me Rachel Lynn."

"Come on in Rachel Lynn! I was hoping you'd be showing up." The voice behind the door sounded weak, yet cheerful.

Joshua looked around the room as they stepped in. It seemed to be a typical girl's room. Frilly curtains and matching bedspread. A few stuffed animals sitting here and there. Brightly colored furniture. A couple posters of some young, boy-band singers on the wall. Just about what he'd expected to see there. What he hadn't expected was the appearance of the girl before him. He knew she was sick, but Rachel Lynn had never told him what she was sick from. Her face was a pale, ashen gray color and had splotches of red here and there too. In fact, the way light from the window shone on her face, you could almost say her skin had a greenish blue tint as well, almost like that of a fish. He didn't really have a chance to think about it much as Rachel Lynn's bouncy personality took over the room at that point.

"It's so good to see you again, Sarah," said Rachel Lynn as she bent over to give her a hug. "I brought along a friend for you to meet, too!"

"I can see that." Sarah smiled a weak smile.

"Sarah, this is my friend, Joshua. Joshua, this is Sarah."

"Pleased to meet you." Both of them answered the other simultaneously.

"Well, it's good to see you two in synch right off the bat! Sarah, this is the guy I told you about before. You know, the one I was going to try and get to come over here and pray for you."

Sarah laughed a weak laugh. "I'd think you were trying to set us up if it weren't for the fact I may not be around much longer."

"Now you just get that talk out of your head, Sarah," answered Rachel Lynn, "you know only the Lord knows how much longer you'll be around."

"Maybe so, but I have a feeling He's going to be telling me about it real soon."

"Hush, you! Cut it out. Don't talk like that."

"Rachel Lynn, I've made my peace with the situation. I'm not afraid."

Rachel Lynn turned her head so Sarah wouldn't see a tear roll down her cheek.

"Mind if I interrupt here?" asked Joshua.

"Go ahead Josh, what do you want to say?" asked Sarah.

"Well," continued Joshua, "it's kind of awkward, but just what exactly is wrong with you?"

"That's the catch. No one knows."

"No one?"

"No one. Believe me, a lot of good doctors took their

best shot at it, but none of them have a clue. They've all tried lots of things, but they all came up empty. The only thing they can all agree on is they think I'm slowly fading away."

"You sound pretty calm about it."

"I wasn't at first. Pretty scared to be honest, but after a while, I came to grips with it. I don't want to go, but I'll get to be with Jesus. I don't know what I'd do if not for Him. I've fought this as best I could, but I'm tired. So tired."

"Well, that's what it's all about. Eternity. This life here is just temporary, but are you sure you're ready to give up on being here so soon?"

"Where'd you find this guy, Rachel Lynn?" Even with a weak voice, it was apparent Sarah was a little annoyed with Joshua's comment.

"Um....Brooksville. I brought him along because I've heard about some miracles they've had at their church. I thought maybe he'd have a different way of praying or something."

"Brooksville, eh? You've seen a genuine miracle there?"

Joshua slowly nodded his head in response to her question without saying a word.

"Did you come here to do a miracle on me?"

Joshua shook his head the other way. The negative motion brought an immediate reaction from Sarah.

"Rachel Lynn, why did you bring him here to do this to me? Give me false hope?"

"I just brought Joshua along to pray with us. I figured it wouldn't hurt."

Sarah raised her voice. "And he's shaking his head no. Crush what little spirit I had left why don't you?"

Joshua had heard enough. "Listen, Sarah. I've already told Rachel Lynn I'm nothing special. I haven't done any miracles and I never will do any miracles. Only God does miracles. I've agreed to pray over you, but if anything happens, it will be God doing it, not me. If nothing happens, it's because it's not in His plan on this day. You seem to be a nice person and I really don't know why things happen to good people, but they do, that's just the reality of the fallen world we live in. Things happen we don't understand. I'm sorry if my being here offends you. If you don't want me to join you in prayer, I won't, but I'm still willing to pray with you if you want."

Sarah started to cry. "I'm sorry. I don't mean to act this way. It's just that sometimes…." Her voice trailed off as she sobbed softly.

Rachel Lynn sat down on the bed beside Sarah and gave her a tight hug. "I'm so sorry, we didn't mean to upset you like this. Really we didn't."

Joshua was touched by the sight of the two friends and prayed silently. He wished God had a clear direction for him here, but he wasn't feeling a thing. He knew he was supposed to be there, but that was all he knew, all he felt. It really hurt to see these two girls sobbing together before him. If only he had a special word or something from the Holy Spirit to make their pain go away and make them happy again. He continued praying, but he still didn't feel any answers. His eyes were still closed in prayer when he felt someone take his hand. He opened his eyes to see Sarah looking up at him, her eyes swollen and red from crying, the visible trails of her tears still on her cheeks, but a smile was now on her face.

"I'm sorry to be such a party-pooper. I know you and Rachel Lynn mean well. Can you forgive me for putting on this little show of weakness?"

"It's alright. You're really not weak, you're stronger than you realize. I don't think I could handle this situation nearly as well as you are."

"Don't be modest, Joshie," Rachel Lynn chimed in, "you're the spiritually strongest person I've ever met. That is why I brought you along, you know."

"I told you I'm not…"

"Yes, yes, I know, you're nothing special," interrupted

Rachel Lynn, "but you seem to have a more open line of communication to God than anyone I've ever been around, even my own pastor."

"I can't do anything that you can't do yourself, Rachel Lynn. Or that Sarah can't do. It seems to me like she's pretty strong in the Spirit herself."

"Hello. Excuse me, sick girl here, pay attention. How about you two quit quibbling and get on with the praying you came here for. I'm not getting any healthier listening to you two argue, you know."

"Oh, I'm so sorry Sarah," answered Rachel Lynn, "I guess we just got a little carried away with our conversation."

"I'll say, I was feeling neglected."

"I'm sorry too," said Joshua sheepishly, "we've just met and I'm already giving you a bad impression."

"Don't sweat it, Joshua. If I can call Rachel Lynn a friend or mine, how picky can I be?" laughed Sarah.

Rachel Lynn just sneered at her and threw a stuffed pig in Sarah's direction.

"Maybe we should just get down to business and do what we came here for," said Joshua, "let's get to praying. Sarah, do you think we could get your sister to join us?"

Sarah looked up at Joshua with obvious sadness on her face and held up the stuffed pig Rachel Lynn had thrown at her. "We'd have a better chance of having this pig fly around the room on its' own."

"Well, I guess it's just up to us then. Rachel Lynn, you place your hands on Sarah's left shoulder and I'll place mine on her right shoulder as we pray for her."

"Is this right Joshua? I've never prayed like this for anyone before."

"It says in the scriptures to lay hands on the sick. That's what we're doing. It's really nothing special on our part. God does all the heavy lifting."

"Are you sure you two know what you're doing? I've never seen anyone pray like this before," said Sarah in a meek voice that showed she was a little unsure of what was going on.

"Well, in the book of Mark it says 'they will lay their hands on the sick, and they will recover.' Sound to me like a good thing to do," explained Joshua. "I know that's how my dad always prays for the sick, and he's had some pretty good results."

"I didn't mean anything by it, it's just that I'm used to having people just say they'd pray for me and leave it at that. I've never had anyone say they'd pray for me and do it while I was present."

"So what you're really saying is that you don't even know for sure if those people prayed for you or if they just said they did?"

"Well. I guess not. I mean, well, I guess when you put it that way, I know I've done that myself. Said I'd pray for someone and never actually got around to it."

Joshua paused, wanting to make sure the right words came out. "I'm not saying that what you're used to is wrong, because it isn't, but I just like to make sure the prayers I pray have as much effect as possible. Sometimes I even feel the power of the Holy Spirit running through me like an electric current when I lay hands on someone and pray for them like this too. Sort of lets me know that God is real and He cares."

"That's pretty wild," said Sarah. Rachel Lynn just stood by without saying a word, her hand still resting on Sarah's left shoulder.

"I don't know if 'wild' is what I'd call it, but it's definitely like nothing you'd experience in ordinary life."

"Well nothing else has worked, so why not? Let's give it a try." Rachel Lynn nodded in agreement.

Joshua got a serious look on his face. "Sarah, before we start, I have to ask you if you have faith that God can heal you if it's part of his plan. Do you believe he will?"

"I guess so. We don't talk about healing too awful much in our church, but I don't see why not."

"Sarah, how can you expect to receive healing if you don't really believe in it?"

"It's just that everyone says God doesn't do miracles like in the Bible any more. What you're talking about here is a miracle. Rachel Lynn told me you've been around miracles, but I figured it was just some sort of coincidence."

"I can assure you the things I've seen haven't been coincidences. No tricks, no smoke and mirrors, or anything else like that. Just God showing up and being God."

"Well, if you say so. I'm in. What have I got to lose?"

"Nothing to lose, everything to gain."

The girls looked at each other, then they both looked at Joshua.

"Let's do this!"

"Okay, let's all agree together in prayer for Sarah's healing."

The two girls prayed silently as Joshua led them in a healing prayer. Sarah opened her eyes and peeked at him several times as he was praying. Not even her pastor looked so intense during a prayer. Maybe God had sent him here just to pray for her. That thought made her smile as she closed her eyes.

2 SHEILA

Joshua had no sooner said "amen" to end their prayer when the front door slammed so loudly they could feel the vibrations clear up to the second floor where Joshua and Rachel Lynn were standing. The slam was shortly followed by the loud voices of an obvious argument and what seemed to be the sound of some sort of glass breaking. Sarah turned her head so she wouldn't have to make eye contact with Joshua or Rachel Lynn. Her embarrassment was obvious. Joshua and Rachel Lynn exchanged puzzled looks as a new sound of stomping feet coming up the stairs filled the room. The suspense of the moment didn't last long as the door to the bedroom flew open and bounced off the wall behind it with a loud thud.

"Alright, mom twisted my arm and made me come up here to meet you people, so hello, nice to meet ya, nice to see ya, I'm outta here."

Rachel Lynn was too stunned to do anything, but Joshua was intrigued by this person that had just burst upon their presence. This girl was not quite the type that he was used to seeing around in his small town. Like the people they had seen outside, she wore tattered clothing that appeared to be tattered by design consisting of a mixture of denim, leather, and chains all topped off with a hair color that could best be described as a burgundy color with a few streaks of silver. Joshua stepped forward with his hand outstretched, trying his best to act as normal as possible in this situation that was obviously anything but normal.

"Pleased to meet you, I'm ..."

The strange girl interrupted abruptly without letting him finish.

"Yes, you should be pleased, or maybe even honored. Handshakes are not requested nor are they necessary."

"Like I was saying, my name is Joshua and ..."

"That's your problem, not mine."

"Sheila!" Everyone's eyes turned towards a very obviously furious and embarrassed Sarah.

"Joshua, if you haven't figured it out yet, this is my sister Sheila. Sheila, you apologize right now, that is no way to treat a guest in our house."

"I didn't mean nuthin' by it."

"Apologize right now."

"For what? Being myself? No way. You guys are a bunch of losers. I only came up here because it was the only way I could get mom to shut up. She told me you guys were up here praying, and praying is for losers. And this preacher-boy here looks like the biggest loser of all. Okay, I've done my time so I can leave now."

"Sheila!" Sarah was starting to quiver with anger, looking visibly weaker from the strength her anger was taking up.

"Hey, it's okay, no problem," said Joshua as he slowly stepped in a strategic spot where the two sisters wouldn't be able to directly look at one another. He remembered how concerned everyone was about Sarah's sister and now he had a front row seat to see what all the concern was about. Maybe this was really why he was here after all.

"Like I was saying, my name's Joshua, Joshua Carson. If you really want to get out of here, how about you and I go for a hike and talk a bit? I know a neat hiking spot not too far from here. Wouldn't take too long to get to."

Sheila Friede wasn't expecting any kind of interaction like this. Usually people that looked so straight-laced like this Joshua person steered away from her. She looked at him closely to see if there was anything there that would give away what he was up to.

"Come on, those fancy boots of yours look like they'd be comfortable to walk in."

She looked down at her boots. Beat up black leather with multiple chains, studs, and buckles attached. She wore them to look tough. Not "comfortable."

"A little exercise and fresh air will do you good. Not only that, it will get you out of here for a little while too."

Rachel Lynn and Sarah exchanged glances. Neither of them had a clue what Joshua was up to. Sheila was taken off guard by this attention and was taken aback just a little.

"Well," said Sheila softly in a voice that was a vast departure from the personality she had just displayed, "I guess we could take a little walk."

Rachel Lynn and Sarah looked at each other with wide-eyed surprise. Did Joshua know what he was getting himself into? Joshua was wondering the same thing himself.

"Well then, it's settled. Let's go get loaded up in the car."

"You get loaded up, loser. I'm not cargo, so I won't be a load. You're just lucky I choose to come along."

As Sheila walked out the door, Joshua turned to look at Sarah. Sarah was shaking her head and making a "crazy" motion to let him know she thought her sister was nuts. Rachel Lynn's expression was full of concern for Sarah coupled with bewilderment for everything that had just taken place. Joshua could sense there was going to be a great deal of prayer necessary for this adventure.

Mrs. Friede was waiting for Joshua at the bottom of the steps, appearing to be a little anxious and embarrassed.

"What's going on Joshua? Is Sheila causing trouble? You don't have to leave because of her."

"It's not that at all, Mrs. Friede. I'm taking her out for a little hike. Just something to get her away from everything, take her mind off of things."

Mrs. Friede stood silently, speechless from what Joshua had told her.

"That is, if it's okay with you, Mrs. Friede. I don't want to overstep my boundaries here. I know you don't know me. If it's a problem, we won't go."

Mrs. Friede paused a moment before answering. "It's not that. I never know any of the people she runs around with. Sarah's friends were always so decent, but Sheila's..."

"It's alright, Mrs. Friede, you don't have to tell me anything."

"It's just that I'm not sure if anyone decent has ever taken the time to spend with her. Quite frankly, this is a bit of a surprise to me. I'm sure you'll take good care of her on the hike."

"The very best I can, Mrs. Friede."

"Thank you so very much. I really do appreciate your spending time with her. I don't know you, but if Rachel Lynn brought you here, you have to be trustworthy. Have a good time."

"I promise to bring Sheila back in one piece, Mrs. Friede."

"I just hope she lets you come back in one piece, Joshua."

"Don't worry, this will just be a fun walk for both of us, Mrs. Friede."

"I surely hope so."

"So do I," Joshua thought to himself. He was starting to have doubts about this whole idea, but it was too late now to turn back. A feeling of dread was starting to fill him as he walked outside and saw Sheila was already sitting in his car waiting on him, window down and arm hanging outside. He had a little bit of a shiver run down his spine as he saw that she had noticed he was coming down the steps to the car and gave him an evil-looking glare. It didn't help that her 'friends' were still there, obviously making fun of him amongst themselves.

"C'mon, c'mon, you're holding up a heavy-duty good time for sure! Get the lead out, preacher-boy!" He cringed a little each time she banged on the side of his car door as she yelled at him. He had a very uneasy feeling about him as he opened his door and got in.

"A little geeky, but not a bad car you got here J. Is it yours?"

"Sort of. I don't really own it, but my father fixed it up for me to use. He's pretty handy with mechanical things. Don't take this the wrong way, but I'd appreciate it if you took your feet off the dash."

He grimaced a little bit as her boots drug across the dash, but it didn't appear as if she had done any real damage to it.

"You'll need to buckle up your seat belt too."

"Hey, don't go all dictator on me now."

"It's the law, you know. Besides, you might break my windshield if I hit something and you're not buckled in."

He shuddered a bit at the evil look she shot at him over that comment.

"I was just making a joke. Sorry. I guess it wasn't all that funny."

"You're right, it wasn't." The coldness in her voice was downright creepy.

"Anyway, it's the law. And it is safer that way too. You never know what might happen down the road."

"Alright, alright, don't get yourself all worked up. I'm bucklin' up. I'm bucklin' up. Let's get goin'.'"

Joshua pulled out as soon as he heard her seat belt buckle click. This ride was just starting and it already felt like it was lasting a long time.

"Lighten up and live a little bit, J-boy. You're wrapped a little too tight."

"Let's straighten out one thing right away. My name's Joshua and that's what my friends call me."

"And what do the people that don't like you call you?"

He wasn't expecting that reply and didn't have an answer to it.

"Have it your way Joshua."

The slow, sneering way she said his name was obviously meant to get on his nerves. It was up to him to not let her see just how well it worked.

"Thank you. This car is old and it isn't much, but I want to try and make it last as long as I can."

"Get a grip, you break it and someone will spring for another one. Old people like to keep us happy you know. Makes 'em feel, you know, useful."

"I don't think that's how it works. We're supposed to be respectful and try to get the most out of what's been given to us."

"I can see you have a lot to learn, Joshua-boy."

He had a feeling if there was anything to be learned from her on this trip, it would be things he didn't really want to know.

"Okay, Sheila. Tell me what you do at school. Play any sports? Belong to any clubs?"

The questions made her laugh so hard that Joshua started to wonder if what he'd said had come out terribly wrong.

"That's a good one, preacher-boy. The only sport I'm involved in is class skipping. And take a real good look at me. Do I look like the type that would be allowed into one of those clubs for losers?"

"I didn't mean anything by…."

"Of course you didn't. Your kind never does. I'm an outcast and I'm okay with that. It's a lot easier to hang out with my kind than to try and get your kind to like me."

"Kind?"

"Yes. Kind. Your kind. You're one of those goody-goods that never do anything wrong. Life's always perfect for you. You're not like us."

"And us is?"

"You know. My crew. The rest of the misfits in school. The ones your mother warned you about. We all stick together because none of the other groups will have anything to do with us."

"I think I know what you mean. There are different groups of kids like that in our school too."

"And you're in the goody-good group, right?"

"I guess that depends on how you look at it. If you mean the group that's always smiling, doing special little favors for the teachers, participating in all the clubs, and never getting into any sort of trouble…well, no, I'm not a part of that group."

"Really? I find that hard to believe. You certainly look the type. You definitely don't have the look of my group. You don't look like a super-nerd or a jock-type. Just what group do you belong to?"

"I don't really belong to what you call a group. I have a circle of Christian friends, but I wouldn't call it a group. Other than our faith, we don't share too many common interests or hang out that much together. I'm a loner most of the time."

"I could tell right away you were a preacher-boy, but I would've never pegged you for the loner type. I guess that's one thing we have in common then."

"Probably the only thing," he thought to himself.

For the first time on this drive, they each ran out of words to say. Joshua kept his eyes on the road, scanning back and forth for wild animals while Sheila took in the scenery along the road. She wasn't used to being out of town much and this drive up into the mountains was taking her mind off of everything that was weighing on it. Sometimes it was tough to keep up her cool, tough front. She felt a bit more comfortable being with this stranger instead of being around everyone who knew her and had their own ideas of how she should act. This Joshua character didn't know her, so that left her free to be whoever she wanted to be. That thought made her smile as Joshua turned the car onto a well-traveled dirt road.

"You're gonna get your car dirty J-boy."

"Nothing a little soap and water won't cure. There's a parking lot back here where we can leave the car while we hike."

"Whatever lights your candle, J-boy."

"Please call me Joshua, okay?"

"Getting a little uptight, are we Joshie?"

The sugary way she imitated Rachel Lynn's voice made the hair on the back of his neck stand up.

Sheila couldn't contain her laughter. "The look on your face! Priceless! I knew that would rub you the wrong way!"

"Ha, ha. Very funny."

"I thought so. Don't worry, Joshua it is. Joshie." Sheila couldn't resist poking fun at him and started laughing some more.

"Thanks, I think. Looks like we're here."

"Yeah. So we are."

3 THE HIKE

Joshua looked around to see if there were any signs of other hikers in the vicinity. It wasn't uncommon for some of them to pitch small tents to spend the night. They had passed one of the prime camping areas on the way in and there was no one there. Others would come by mountain bike. On this day, he wasn't able to find any signs of any other people around. No cars, bikes, or tents anywhere to be seen. He was still looking around when he heard a snapping sound next to him that caused him to turn his head towards it.

"What in the…."

The volume of his voice rose before he became speechless. Of all the things his mind expected to see, one of them was not the sight of the girl beside him unfastening the snaps on her blouse. It seemed like his hands contained only thumbs as he rapidly fought with the door handle to get out of the car as quickly as he could. It was so fast and so awkward that he tumbled to the ground when the door opened. He was still in such a rush to get out of the car, that he half rolled, have crawled away.

"Joshua Carson! You get back here! Come back here! You get back here right now!"

The tone of Sheila's voice scared him a little bit. It sounded like a cross between desperation and anger. He tried to remain calm, but his voice shook as he replied.

"What do you think you're doing, Sheila?"

"What do you think I'm doing? Isn't this why you brought me here?" Her voice was anything but calm, beginning to sound almost frantic.

"Uh, no." He tried to keep his voice from shaking this time, but had no luck.

"Then what did you bring me here for anyway? Aren't I pretty enough for you? Suddenly think you're too good for me?" She continued cursing at him under her breath and her voice started to break. It sounded to him like she might be starting to cry, too. As threatening and broken as it was, the sound of her voice breaking had a strange, calming effect on him and he was able to get over his shaky voice and spoke in reassuring tone.

"I told you before we left what we came here for. Just to talk and take a little bit of a hike. That's all. No more, no less. You're a very attractive girl, but I'm not about to do anything to you like that. That's not what we're here for and I'm not after anything more. It's not right for me or anyone else to treat you like some sort of object. You're much too special to be treated that way. All girls are."

"You don't know what you're talking about." She began to sob openly before him. "I'm not special at all. I'm just a piece of trash. Just ask anyone."

"I will say you are a bit on the different side, but that doesn't make you any less special. God made you and He doesn't make junk."

The following silence was awkward, but he was still afraid to turn around to face her. He could hear a lot of sniffling and snorting going on behind him, so he hoped Sheila was getting herself back together. It was only a moment till he heard the car door slam and he turned to see that she had, in fact, not only gotten herself composed, but was looking just as rough and surly as ever. He felt a slight shiver running up and down his back as she came over and looked him squarely in the eye.

"You're weird, you know that?"

"Uh, well,…"

"Oh, close your trap before you attract flies. Let's get started on this hike you talked about."

"Okay, let me get my backpack out of the trunk."

He breathed a sigh of relief as he stuck his head in the trunk of his car. With that uncomfortable incident behind them, maybe they could both relax. Maybe he could unravel the mystery that was Sheila Friede.

"Whoa, cool backpack! Where did you get it?"

"It's my father's. He used to do a lot of camping on the road and thought I could use it for hiking."

"Your father's?" Her face showed a look of obvious bewilderment.

"Yeah. This backpack has been around."

"You said he did a lot of camping on the road, but I thought I heard Sarah and Rachel Lynn whispering about your dad being a preacher. Preachers and camping out on the road don't seem to go together. That backpack doesn't look like something a preacher would own."

"You can't judge a book by its' cover, but you are right. My dad wouldn't own anything like this."

"I don't get it. You just said…"

"But my father would."

"Wait just one minute here, bub. You can't have it both ways."

"Well, let's just say all the branches in my family tree aren't straight."

"I don't get it. What do you mean?"

"I have a dad and a father. My father left before I was born. My dad adopted me after he married my mom. Not too long ago, my father came back into my life, so I have both a dad and a father now."

"You're twice as lucky as me then."

"Now it's my turn not to get it. What do you mean?"

"I don't have a dad or father. My dad died when I was little. Some people say I'm like him, but I don't really remember him so I don't know."

"I'm sorry to hear that."

"Don't be. We managed to get by. It was always easier for Sarah, though. It's like she and my mother think with one brain or something because they're so much alike. I was always the odd-ball, the black sheep of the family."

"Seems to me that you work hard to live up to that image too."

"Why you…"

Her sentence turned into a tirade of foul language like he'd never heard coming from the mouth of anyone before, let alone a teenage girl. It was an awkward moment for him. None of the other girls he knew had an edge to them like Sheila. He admired how strong-willed she was, but the language coming out of her mouth was definitely something he found very unattractive and he was starting to question the wisdom behind even suggesting this hike. "Maybe the best thing to do is just stand here and wait till she runs out of words," he thought to himself. It looked like she was finally winding down.

"Well?"

"Uh, well what?"

"I just ripped into you and called you every dirty name I could think of, plus I made a couple more up just for the fun of it, and you're just standing there saying nothing. It's your turn to yell right back at me. That's how we fight."

"I don't want to fight and I'm not here to fight. We're just here to have a friendly hike. If you want to fight you'll have to find someone else to hike with."

"I don't get you. Some of the guys I've been with would've slapped me for yelling at them like that."

"I'm not other guys and maybe you should consider changing the kind of guy you hang out with."

That was a thought that hadn't really entered her mind before. Maybe she had been looking for all the wrong things in a guy. This guy Joshua appeared to be softer and weaker than the guys she dated and hung around, yet there was a strength in him that she just couldn't put her finger on. It was a strength that attracted her to him, yet scared her a little at the same time. The curiosity of the whole thing was making her a bit more attentive to him than she had ever imagined.

"Well, yeah," she said in meek manner that surprised her when she heard it coming from her own mouth, "you may be on to something." She couldn't let that meek tone continue, so she immediately threw up the fence around herself again and put the tougher edge back out front.

"Anyway, just what is it we're out here to see anyway?"

"There's a lot of neat old stuff out here. I've always enjoyed seeing the old remnants of days gone by."

"Yeah, you seem like someone who came from a long time ago. You certainly don't belong here in this time."

"Whatever you say," laughed Joshua, "I don't claim this world as my home anyway."

"I'd ask what you mean by that, but I'm not in the mood for a sermon."

He could tell by the smirk on her face not to push her on that last comment. "Let's just get going on this hike, okay? I think you'll enjoy it."

"Yeah, sure. We may as well start so we can get it over with."

"I can almost smell your enthusiasm."

"That's just the tuna sandwich I had for lunch, smart guy. Let's get going."

"If it's alright with you, I'd like to show you something that's off of a trail down the road here."

"Oh, like I have a choice? Is that how it is? I don't know any of this hiking stuff or what's around here, so I'm going to leave it pretty much up to you, Josie."

"Joshua."

"Yeah, whatever."

"Let's get started. It's just a short bit down this way."

The two of them started walking down the gravel road from the parking lot. Joshua took in all of the scenery and mentally made notes of the types of trees they were passing and kept his eyes open for any wildlife that might be visible along the way. Sheila mostly just kicked the stones as they walked.

"Here's the trail I wanted to show you. Let's go this way now."

"The trail sign says 'Railroad Arch' on it. Is that the big surprise you have in store, just an old railroad arch?"

"It's really pretty cool, Sheila. I bet you've never seen anything like it before."

"I've never seen the Queen of England either, but that doesn't make her cool."

"Just stick with me, I think you might end up enjoying yourself just a little."

"Well, I don't…hey, is that a cat over there?"

"No, that's a fox."

"A fox? A real, live, wild animal type fox?"

"Yes, and if we're lucky, we may see some other animals too."

Joshua could see the effect the little fox had on Sheila. It was obvious that she was the type that never spent any time in the wilderness. It was obvious there was a lot more to Sheila than anyone ever knew before.

"Wait!"

"What?"

"Do you really want to see some more animals?"

"Well, I guess so. That little fox was so cute!"

"How about a fish?"

"A fish?"

"Yes, a fish. That's a trout hiding under that tree root along the stream bank right there. Do you see it?"

"Wow! I do see it, I do! This is the first time I've ever seen a fish that wasn't on a dinner plate."

For the first time since he met her, Joshua saw Sheila's tough outer shell soften. A genuine smile came across her face when she saw the fish. Maybe there was some hope for her after all.

"Pretty cool, isn't it? I told you this hike would be fun. Just give it a chance, and I think you'll actually enjoy yourself."

"We'll see. Do we have to go across that little bridge over there?"

"Yep. Just be careful, it's kind of narrow and we don't want you falling in. It might scare the fish."

"Oh aren't you suddenly the comedian?"

Sheila suddenly felt something different. It was the smile on her face. She couldn't remember the last time she smiled or the last time someone was able to make her smile. It felt kind of good for a change. It was also nice to get away and leave everything behind. Some days, between the weight of being a troublemaker and dealing with her sister's illness, she felt like she could barely get by. Now away from all that, and being with someone who was able to make her smile, almost made her feel like dancing. This little hike was surely something she needed. This guy Joshua was a little strange with all the church stuff he would talk about, but it was getting to be fun following along behind him on the trail and seeing all the things he pointed out along the way.

"That thing up ahead. Is that the arch thing you wanted me to see?"

"Yes, that's it. One of the hidden wonders of the area. Most people around here don't even know it's here."

"It looks like some sort of bridge, but I've never seen anything like it before."

"It is pretty special. Old, too. I've heard that all the stones they used to make it came from right around here. They were trying to make some kind of railroad bed through here and brought in a bunch of stone masons from Italy to build these things. Look at it real close. See how well those stones fit together? You won't find craftsmanship like that anywhere today. They put all those stones together so many years ago and this thing is still solid, even though no one looks after it at all."

"Things like this get you excited, don't they?" Sheila laughed a little as she pointed that little fact out to him.

"I don't know about excited," laughed Joshua, "but I do find it fascinating. The tunnel we're going to was also originally built for the same railroad."

"Tunnel?"

"Yes, a tunnel. That's where we're hiking to from here. They never did finish the railroad, but the tunnel was used as part of the super highway near here. It was abandoned back around 1970 when they changed the course of the road a bit."

"An abandoned tunnel sounds a little creepy to me."

"Some people probably do find it to be on the creepy side. I think it's as fascinating as this arch here and I think you'll enjoy it even more."

They didn't say much as they walked down the gravel road to the path that led down to the old, abandoned road leading to the tunnel. Joshua noticed on the way to the arch Sheila made a point of kicking a lot of stones on the gravel road, probably out of nervousness. On the way back he noticed she hadn't been kicking the stones nearly as much. He hoped she was becoming more comfortable with him and ready to talk about the things going on in her life. They hadn't gone far down the tattered highway when she began to open up.

"You're a big church guy, aren't you Joshua?"

"Not really, our church is kind of on the small side."

"That's not what I meant, I mean you're big into going to church all the time, aren't you? I kind of gathered that from all that praying you were doing at our house."

"I'm not quite sure where you're headed with this, but yes, I do go to church."

"And you believe in all that church mumbo-jumbo, right?"

"I believe in what we do and who we're living for, but I

wouldn't call it mumbo-jumbo."

"Well, there's just a couple things I'm confused about. Maybe you can help me out and explain it all to me since you're a church guy. I think my sister's going to die soon. I heard about you guys praying for her and listened to what you were saying about healing."

"How in the world did you hear that? You weren't in the room."

"I snuck in the back door. There's a vent in Sarah's room that leads to the room I was in downstairs. I could hear every word. When I had enough, I went back outside and came in again so I could yell at my mom a bit."

"Oh, I see. Do you eavesdrop like that often?"

"That's none of your business. So, anyway, what do you think? Will she live or die?"

"It's in God's hands whether she lives or dies and when it happens. Same for all of us."

"That's what I want to ask you about. You believe God knows all and sees all, am I right?"

"In a nutshell, yes."

"And He's supposed to be a loving God that cares for us, right?"

"Well, yes, of course he does."

"That's why I'm mad at Him, if he exists at all."

"Mad? Why?"

"How can a God that's supposed to care about us let my sister get sick? I mean, she's the good one, she doesn't deserve it. If anyone deserves death it's me, not her. She's a perfect angel. Me, I'm altogether different. I've done lots of bad things. I'll probably keep on doing bad things. It's me that deserves to die, not her. To top it off, the way I understand it, He already knows how it's going to end. It's like we're puppets down here, just acting out his little play with no say in anything."

The combination of pain and anger in her voice let him know that he better choose his next words very carefully.

"I think you're talking about predestination."

"Yeah, pre-whatever. I think I've heard that word before. Nothing really matters if it's already decided then, does it? I mean, it's already decided, so what's the point? Unless there is no God. Maybe that's how it is. Maybe we live, we die, and then there's nothing."

"That's not what I believe."

"Yeah, I know. You believe in the grand puppet-master."

"That's not quite how I see it."

"Oh, so you really don't think He knows everything then?"

"I do, but not the way you're putting it. You're leaving out an important element. Free will."

"Free will?"

"Yeah. You chose to come along on this hike. You didn't have to. You made your own choice. Your own free will. He allows us to choose whether we follow Him or not."

"So he didn't know if I was going to come along or not?"

"Well, yes. The Bible tells us that He knows us before we're even born. He knows everything from the beginning of time till the end of it."

"I don't get it, the whole time thing. How He can know all that stuff."

"I have trouble grasping it too, sometimes. God's ways are so much higher than our own that our understanding of how he does things usually falls pretty short. Someone once told me that God sits in a place that's above time and can see it all from beginning to end all at once. Sort of like it's on a giant table in front of him. The way I came to grips with the whole free will thing is imagining that God can not only see what we're going to do, He can also see every path from every decision we make every day."

"Huh?"

"Kind of like we come to a fork in the road and God knows what will happen in either direction before we make

31

the decision which way to go. The same with every decision we make, He already knows what will come out of each choice we make, regardless of the choice."

"Can you hear yourself talking? Do you know how crazy that sounds?"

"If you measure it against normal human life, yes, it does sound pretty crazy. But it's no more crazy than realizing that mankind rebelled against God by not following Him and still believes that He should give them riches and perfect health all the time no matter what they do. With no effort on their part, to boot."

"You're weird. Crazy and weird. I'm beginning to wish I hadn't come along."

"Yet you did. I think God has something special for you to learn from this hike. Your sister has a great inner strength and I see an inner strength in you, too."

"How can she be strong? She's so weak and close to death and you're saying she's strong?"

"She has God's light shining from her heart. The world sees her as weak, but God sees her as strong."

"I don't have a clue what you're talking about."

"She has a strong spirit. It says in the Bible that our wealth is in earthen jars of clay. That's how your sister is, her body is very weak on the outside, but inside her spirit is very strong. That way the world can see that our real power and strength come from Him and not from ourselves."

"Whatever. Maybe you should be in a jar."

4 THE TUNNEL BECKONS

"What's that sound I'm hearing, smart boy?"

"That's the traffic on the superhighway. There's a lot of moisture in the air and sound carries farther on days like this."

"I was just joking. I wasn't expecting you to prove you were a geek."

"Sorry to not disappoint you," laughed Joshua.

Sheila replied with a lot of words that Joshua didn't really care to hear.

"Just how much further do we have to go to reach this thing anyway?"

"It's not far. If it weren't for the way the road curves up ahead, we could probably see it from here."

The two kept walking silently. Sheila had her attention drawn to some graffiti painted on the road by a small pile of half-burnt firewood when a pair of bicyclers zipped by within a few feet of them.

"You lousy good for nothing…."

Sheila's language deteriorated from there as she quickly grabbed some rocks to throw at the bicyclers.

"Hey, settle down, settle down. They weren't that close when they went by."

"Close enough."

She added a few more words under her breath that made him cringe inside.

"Why do you have to be this way?" he asked, his voice unable to hide his growing frustration with her.

"What way? This is just who I am."

"I don't believe that. The cursing person I see before me isn't like the one who was watching the fox with me back on the trail."

"Well, that was just a weak moment. I have to be tough to get by in this world."

"Well there is someone who can bear your burdens so you don't have to be so tough."

Sheila paused and looked down at the ground thoughtfully before answering.

"Look, Carson. I've enjoyed this so far, but I know where you're heading. I'll make you a deal. I'll try to clean up my language for the rest of this hike if you quit trying to push that Jesus guy on me all the time. Deal?"

Sheila's proposal caught Joshua off guard. He knew there was a reason for this hike, a chance to reach Sheila with the gospel message, but maybe it just wasn't going to happen the way he thought. Maybe God had another plan.

"Okay. Deal."

"Well, I didn't expect that to be so easy."

"Believe me, it's not what I wanted or expected, but if it's that important to you, that's how it will be."

"Great! Now maybe we can just enjoy ourselves."

The next few minutes were quietly uneventful, neither of them speaking as they rounded the sweeping turn in the roadway. The turn was always his favorite part of the hike because going around it would gradually reveal the mouth of the tunnel.

Sheila was the first to speak. "Say, I think we're at that tunnel of yours."

"Yes, that's it up ahead in all its' glory."

"Looks kind of like a big hole in the ground."

Joshua started laughing. "What do you think a tunnel is, anyway? You'll see more than a hole when we get closer."

The decaying pavement was getting a little sturdier as they got nearer to the entrance. Off to the right were a few remnants of what was probably a small campfire, probably built for a little warmth. The number of bottles lying around the remains were evidence that more than one person was huddled around the fire. Aging, well-worn concrete barriers were covered with all sorts of graffiti, as was portions of the roadway. Sheila could feel a cool, moist breeze coming from the mouth of the tunnel as they grew nearer to it.

"Looks kind of creepy. That makes it way cool!"

"I've always thought it was pretty cool. Some of the graffiti here makes it creepy."

"You don't like the pictures?"

"Oh, I think some of them show a remarkable talent. A wasted talent, but a real talent nonetheless. I could never come close to doing anything that artistic. Just look in the detail in that cartoon character there! And that demon's head over there looks very lifelike. It's seeing some of the vulgarity and evil that some of these pictures are centered around that makes it feel a little creepy. That and imagining the poor people who use this as the highlight of their lives. I think it's pretty sad. Look at this one here. This poor guy couldn't even spell his foul language correctly."

"Yeah. It is pretty sad. Especially sad since I know that guy. He's one of our gang."

"Oh, I'm sorry. I'm not trying to say that you're sad like him or bring you down."

"No, it's alright," said Sheila in a soft, quiet voice, "before you pointed that out, I never stopped to think just how sad some of the people I hang out with really are. If they aren't doing stuff like this, they can be downright depressing to be around."

"Well, I hope you don't find me depressing to be around."

"Hardly. You're not depressing at all. Just weird. Very, very weird."

"Flattery will get you nowhere. Hard to imagine this place was once swarming with cars and people all the time isn't it?"

"Yeah, it looks kind of haunted with all those windows broken out up there."

"It does look kind of spooky. I doubt there are any ghosts of the former workers on duty, though."

"If these doors weren't blocked shut, we'd go up there and check it out."

"I was up there before the doors were closed up. Not much to see. Pretty much just empty rooms and more graffiti."

"I'm not surprised. I know a lot of the guys in the gang talk about coming up here and partying all night. I'm sure they're behind a lot of it."

"Enough talking about that kind of stuff. Are you ready to go into the tunnel, Sheila?"

"I guess so. I have to admit this is more fun than I thought it would be."

"Good! I'm glad you're enjoying yourself!"

"I didn't say I was enjoying myself, I said it was more fun than I thought it would be. Since I didn't think it would be any fun at all, that's not really saying much."

"You're a tough one, Sheila, you're a tough one."

"Well, you're finally learning something from me instead of the other way around. You do have a light for this don't you? It looks pretty dark."

"I always like to experience it in the dark just for kicks. It's like being in a long cave."

"Whoa, Joshie's livin' on the wild side!"

Joshua just shook his head and started walking into the tunnel. "Be sure to walk in short steps so you don't trip over anything. There shouldn't be anything there, but you never know what someone might have left behind recently."

Sheila's first steps were a little hesitant, but she soon starting walking faster so she wouldn't be too far from Joshua. There was no way she was going to let him find out just how scared she really was of walking through the dark. Being closer to him helped ease her anxiety and boost her confidence so she'd have some swagger left when they came out into the light again.

"Isn't this a little dangerous?"

"You're the one who said we're living on the wild side." Joshua laughed at his own little joke.

"It just looks like we're walking into a whole lot of nothing ahead."

"Sort of like walking into eternity without Jesus."

"Just can't pass up a chance to preach at me, can you?"

"I'm sorry. I didn't mean to preach at you, it's just the first thing that comes into my mind whenever I walk through here without any lights."

"You're weird. The first thing that comes to my mind is wondering if a part of the ceiling is going to fall down on my head."

"I've known more than one person afraid to come in here for the same reason."

"I can believe that. I can't see anything now. It's totally dark before us and totally dark behind us. It would be pretty scary for weak-minded people."

"Yeah, well, most people do bring lights. That's the easy way. I prefer the straight and narrow path less traveled."

Sheila kicked a stone that echoed loudly as it bounced into the darkness against the tunnel floor before stopping in a puddle of water.

"Are you really sure this is safe? We're not walking blindly into a pond or some sort of underground river are we?"

"If I didn't know better, I'd say you're starting to sound

like one of those weak-minded people," laughed Joshua.

"I'd smack you a good one if I could only see where you were at."

"I'm sure you would. Don't worry, I've been through here many times, in the light and in the dark, and there's never been anything to be afraid of. Unless, of course, you're afraid of the dark."

"You'd just better watch your back when it gets light enough for me to see you, Joshie-boy."

"Hey, don't worry, we'll be in the light soon. See how the sunlight is starting to reflect off of the ceiling."

Sheila looked up, and sure enough, there was a glow ahead of them. Not the end of the tunnel like she expected to see, but it was light nonetheless.

"Why are we seeing this glowing light instead of the end of the tunnel?"

"Because it's so long and there's a bit of an arc to the road. As soon as we get to the high point, we'll be able to see the end of the tunnel."

"Good. I'm not scared at all, but I am getting a little creeped out by all this darkness."

Joshua could hear a little bit of fear sneaking into her voice, but he knew better than to point it out to her.

"See up ahead? The mouth of the tunnel is visible now. It will keep getting lighter now as we go."

"Yeah, I see it. It's about time."

Sheila was relieved to see the mouth of the tunnel. She wouldn't dare let on how much being in total darkness had unnerved her for some reason.

"Hey, Joshua, does it always look this way? There's something strange about how it looks."

"It looks like there's some sort of fog near the entrance. Not really unusual given all the dampness that's in here and how hot the sunlight outside can get. I've seen fog around the mouth of the tunnel before, but it does seem to have a different kind of look to it this time. Almost like it's glowing a little bit."

The fog swirled around them in a mesmerizing way as they continued towards the mouth of the tunnel. Sheila wouldn't admit it to Joshua, but she found it to be beautiful. Joshua wouldn't admit it to Sheila, but he found it strange and unusual. Almost to the point it scared him. They were both secretly relieved to walk out of the tunnel into the light.

"See? There was nothing to be afraid about. We made it out in one piece, no problem."

"Oh, were you afraid, Joshie? I wasn't. Looks like this end of the tunnel is pretty much the same as the other one. Seems to be in a little worse shape, though."

"Well, yeah, there's not much difference from one end to the other. That's why I think the real experience is to walk the whole way through with no lights. It makes the journey kind of special."

"Say, what's that thing over there? Looks like some sort of tombstone. Is someone buried up here?"

Joshua stopped in his tracks. As many times as he'd been here, he'd never noticed the marker Sheila was asking about before. Confusion entered his mind as he tried to rationalize how he could've missed something this big that had obviously been there for some time. He was so entranced by this puzzle that he wasn't able to answer Sheila as he slowly stepped toward it.

"Hey what's going on, Joshua? Why'd you suddenly go quiet?"

Joshua looked up and down at the monument that he now stood next to. It was slightly taller than him, coming to a point at the top, and was made of the same kind of material as a tombstone. There was a little graffiti, but no writing on the side he was on, so he began to walk around it to see if there was any on one of the other sides. For some reason, he was relieved to find words on the next side. He silently mouthed the words as he read; IN MEMORY OF THE LOST CHILDREN OF THE TUNNEL.

The inscription puzzled him. He never heard of anyone going missing around the tunnel. Surely he would have heard something, even a tale from the old-timers if it had happened long ago. It appeared as if there was some more writing down lower that was covered by branches and leaves so he began to brush it away to see if there were any more clues about this monument. The base was very dirty, so he had to wipe some of the dirt away from the words that were beginning to show with the debris out of the way.

Sheila was watching Joshua closely as he surveyed the monument. The ever-present confidence he displayed seemed to have vanished as he started studying it. It was obvious he found some writing on it and she was fascinated by how intense he appeared to be as he read it. He started to look a little nervous as she watched him clear debris away from the base of the stone and become almost frantic as he was wiping it off to read. Suddenly she saw his face turn as white as a ghost and jump back from the monument so fast that it almost looked like the stone itself had thrown him back.

"Joshua! What's wrong?"

"Look." His voice shook a bit as he spoke. "Look at the words."

Sheila came closer and started to read the inscription on the stone. "You may no longer be with us, but we'll always love you and remember you always ..." Sheila's voice dropped off to a whisper, "Joshua Carson and Sheila Friede."

Sheila's knees trembled and she dropped to the ground.

"Joshua. How? ?Why? What does this mean?"

Joshua's voice was still shaking. "Look. Look at the last line. Look at the date."

A gasp escaped from Sheila's throat as she read the date. "Joshua. That's today's date. What's going on here Joshua? What's going on?" Sheila was becoming frantic.

"I don't know. I don't know."

"I want to go home." The fear in her voice was obvious.

"Yeah. Me too."

Joshua helped her to her feet and together they walked through the swirling, glowing mist that was surrounding the mouth of the tunnel.

5 THE ADVENTURE BEGINS

"I'm scared, Joshua. Can we please use a light this time?"

"Sheila, I'm pretty scared myself. Someone has to be playing some sort of trick on us, but I can't imagine who would go to such trouble or why."

"I just want to go home and forget all this. I wish you had never brought me here in the first place."

"I'm sorry. I wish I hadn't come here myself right now. But there has to be a logical explanation for all of this."

"Sure. Right. When you figure it out, tell me about it. Better yet, send me a postcard so I don't have to look at you again."

Sheila was trying to put up a brave front, but Joshua could tell by her voice that she was really scared. He definitely couldn't hold that against her, because he was feeling pretty scared himself. There was really something wrong about what was going on and the fact that he had no clue about it concerned him more than anything.

"Hey, there really can't be anything to it, right? I mean, someone just has to be playing a joke on us. We'll come out the other end of this tunnel and just go back home. Then maybe we can track down the prankster that put that fake monument up." He hoped that explanation sounded better than it felt.

"Yeah, when I get ahold of them……"

All of the foul language that was coming out of Sheila's mouth didn't bother Joshua so much this time. Her temper brought things back to normal for the moment and it was actually more of a comfort to him, not offensive.

"I'm not sure some of the things you're suggesting to do to our pranksters are anatomically possible, but this is one time I won't stand in your way. Just remember to repent of your sins after you're done, okay?"

Joshua's joke made Sheila feel at ease and she began to laugh.

"You're even weirder than I thought, Joshua. But I'm starting to like your style."

"We can discuss style points on the way home. I can finally see the end of the tunnel, and I don't know about you, but I'm ready to get out of here."

"Yeah, me too. Hey, it looks like that funky fog is around this end of the tunnel now too, Joshua."

"Just another bit of strangeness I'll be happy to leave behind today. It's so thick at this end, I can't really see through it."

"I'm not sure if I like this any better than when we were in complete darkness."

"Here. Take my hand so we stay together and we'll just walk straight ahead. This will all be gone once we're outside."

"Sure you want to hold my hand on the first date, Joshie-woshie?"

The sugary sweetness of Sheila's voice as she teased him was so comical they both began to laugh.

"Just be thankful I'm a gentleman. There, the fog is starting to thin out now that we're outside. Just a little bit further and ..."

Joshua's words caught in his throat and he was speechless. Sheila uttered one loud profanity and she too, was speechless. They both gazed open-mouthed and wide-eyed at what lay before them. It was only a few moments before Sheila composed herself enough to speak, but it felt like hours for both of them. Even then, her voice was still weak and squeaky."

"Joshua. Joshua what happened to the road? Shouldn't there be a road here?""

Joshua was still in a confused state. What should have been an abandoned roadway was instead a forest. No clearing, no trails, no signs of civilization at all. He felt even more confused as he turned to survey their surroundings.

Joshua raised his arms and screamed skyward, "Father in Heaven, what is going on?"

The fear in his voice scared Sheila more than anything else had to this point. He had been calm the whole day through whatever was going on and now he was freaking out.

"Hey, calm down. I'm supposed to be the one that can't handle things, not you."

"Sheila. Look around. Not only is there no more road, there's no more tunnel. The tunnel we just came out of is gone."

Sheila had only been looking forward for a road. Now she turned around and discovered, just as Joshua had, they were surrounded by forest. There was absolutely nothing around. The shock of it all was more than she could bear and she began to cry.

"Now, now, just settle down, we'll get this figured out."

"How can we?" she sobbed, "there's nothing here to figure out. It's all gone."

"Settle yourself down, and get quiet. We'll just listen for the nearest traffic and walk towards the road."

The two of them huddled together and was as quiet as they could be.

"I don't hear anything Joshua."

"Neither do I. This just isn't right. I once heard there

were only a few places left on earth where you couldn't hear human activity, yet I don't hear a thing. Nothing. Just some birds and the wind rustling through the leaves."

"You don't suppose ... suppose ..." Sheila's voice trailed off into a scared whisper, unable to finish her sentence.

"Suppose what?"

"Suppose that everyone else in the world is gone. That there's no one left but us."

"Sheila, I really don't know what to think. I don't think that is the case, but I don't really have an answer to any of this."

"I thought you were the one that always had all the answers."

Joshua tried to speak, but no words came out. The realization he had been allowing himself to take credit for knowing so much when he really should have been giving credit to God all along hit him right in his spirit and the feeling really hurt. At the same time, he realized he was letting fear run rampant within himself. He knew the spirit of fear didn't come from God, yet he allowed everything that had been going on lead him into fear and despair. Relying on his own wisdom had led him to a dead end where he was lost in all his fears. He knew now the One he had to turn to for answers to make it all right again.

"Sheila, I'm sorry I misled you. Everything I know I have to give God the glory for teaching me those things. I've been running scared through this because I've been trusting my own self and not seeking His direction. Now, if you'll excuse me, I need to get into some serious prayer to see what we need to do about this mess."

"Yeah, right. While you're there talking to the air, I'll fire up my cell phone and get ahold of someone to come get us. In all the excitement, I had forgotten all about it. Modern technology will give us what we need!"

"Okay. You do what you think you need to do, and I'll be over here doing what I know I need to be doing."

Joshua found a large rock to kneel beside while he

prayed. He imagined himself looking much like the classic painting of Jesus praying in the Garden of Gethsemane in that position, and it was ironic thinking that he'd be calling out to God for answers much the same way that Jesus did. A chill went up his spine when his imagination gave him a brief mental image of himself hanging on a cross like Jesus. He became so lost momentarily in the tremendous amount of torture Jesus suffered for him personally that he forgot all about the predicament he and Sheila were in. At least he forgot about it till a very loud string of obscenities from her mouth reached his ears. He took that as a sign her faith in technology saving them had just taken a serious setback. He concentrated on finishing his prayer to help block out the obscenities that were still coming out of her mouth non-stop. He didn't receive an overwhelming answer to his prayer, but now he not only felt much calmer having given his fear over to God, he also had a pretty good idea what they had to do next.

"How did your cell phone work out for you?"

Sheila answered after several rather pointed obscenities. "No signal at all. Nothing. I know I had a full signal before we started out because I checked. Now nothing. Not even GPS because there's no satellite signal to go by either. It's like we dropped off the face of the earth or something."

"Well, if we're not on earth anymore, we're on a planet that's pretty much the same."

"I swear, if I knew you and I weren't the only people left on earth, I'd deck you right now."

"That's just your fear talking, Sheila. I have a feeling everything will be alright in the end."

"Great. A feeling. You have a feeling. You know what I have, buddy? I have a headache from all this stress and if you're not careful, I'll be sharing it with you the hard way."

"Just settle down. What we need to do is gather up some kindling and wood so we can make a fire. It will be dark soon and with no sense of where we are or where anyone else is, it's best that we just settle in for the night and look at it all fresh in the morning."

"That's the grand scheme you got from your pray-thing over there?"

"Yes, but if you have a better idea, I'm all ears."

"Fine. We'll do your campfire thing. But so help me, if you start singing campfire songs, you're dead meat."

"I promise not to sing to you, okay?"

"See that you don't."

The warmth of the fire was comforting, a comfort both of them needed. Joshua kept trying to put Sheila at ease, to help her relax, but he had no luck. He couldn't blame her, either. The only thing that kept him from losing all control was his faith. He tried to share that faith with her, give her something to hold on to, something to believe in, but each time he tried, she stopped him short with a fierce string of obscenities. He knew it was only her fear talking so he didn't give up, but her fear and stubbornness wouldn't budge. After time, they both fell asleep from exhaustion.

Sheila's sound sleep of exhaustion was interrupted by a strong smell that was irritating her nostrils. Her nose twitched back and forth a few times and her head turned in her sleep in a fruitless effort to escape the stench before her eyes opened. The sight that filled her vision was much like the many horror movies she had seen, but this one was reality, not an image on a screen. Her mind was still foggy from sleep, but it soon solved the puzzle of the smell that had awakened her. In the dim glow of the campfire, she could make out the face of a man smiling above her. The putrid smell seemed to be coming from his mouth and the blackened and missing teeth seemed to back that theory up. His dirty, unkempt face and long, stringy hair only seemed to add to the intensity of the smell coming from him. Only the grimy hand clamped tightly over her mouth as soon as her eyes opened prevented her wakening scream from becoming reality. His weight now had her pinned helplessly on the ground, unable to move.

"Ah, lass, it's good to see you finally waking up. I've

been admiring you for a time, I have." The leering tone of his voice sickened her.

"You'll be my friend now, won't you, lassie?"

Pushing with all her strength, Sheila was able to momentarily break his grip and get her mouth away from his hand.

"Joshua!"

Her eyes saw Joshua by the fire as she turned her head to yell. She was gripped by complete terror as she saw Joshua's motionless head turned towards the fire, a heavy stream of blood flowing over his face.

"Oh, I'm sorry, miss, I don't mean to disappoint you now, but I think your young friend won't be joining us. Seems quite content to lay there dead to the world, he does." The cackling laughter that followed his words chilled Sheila to the bone. This horrid man had killed Joshua and she would probably be next.

"Yes, dearie, you're just the prettiest thing my eyes have seen for a long time. Your clothes are a wee bit strange, but I don't mind, no, not one bit."

She cringed as she felt the slobbers from his mouth dripping on her cheek. The stench of his breath as he was breathing on her was making her stomach turn. She knew what he had in mind and she also knew he was too strong for her to do anything about it. Her survival instincts kicked in, trying to think of a happy place for her mind to travel to while this horrid thing was going to happen. Her eyes clenched shut as tightly as they could and her body braced itself against him as she began to think of happy thoughts to fill her mind. Just as she was using all her will to concentrate on a sunny ocean beach, her imagination was interrupted by a loud noise that resembled the sound of a baseball bat smacking against a large watermelon, only there was something different about it. It was only when she realized the disgusting man's weight was no longer on her that she opened her eyes.

"My apologies, missy, this one slipped away from us on

his own for a bit. I suspected he was a bad'n, and this proves it. We'll take care of 'im, we will."

She sat up, and surveyed the scene around her, unable to move from the intensity of everything that had just happened and from the strange scene of people before her now. Her attacker appeared to be unconscious and she could now understand by seeing the blood pouring from his head that the noise she had heard had come from his head being hit, probably by the stock of one of the rifles the men were carrying. A couple men were tying his limp body up and by the rough way they were treating it, they obviously didn't care for him very much. Another man was looking over Joshua and seemed to be treating him like a doctor would although he looked nothing like a doctor. All of them dressed and looked very much like the re-enactors from the old frontier village back home, except their clothes looked more worn and tattered than the re-enactors clothes ever did. The one who had spoken to her began to speak some more.

"We weren't expectin' anyone else to be out here with us. Lucky for you we caught ol' Caleb before he could do any more harm."

Still unable to speak, Sheila just nodded at him. She started to look around at the men, studying them, trying to get some sort of bearing to give her a clue, something explainable to cling to in this world of madness that was holding her prisoner. But still nothing seemed to make any sense at all. Not only were these men strangely dressed, they all had their faces blackened as well, as if they were trying to hide in the dark or something. Had they fallen into the hands of some sort of criminals on the run? The look on her face must have betrayed her thoughts.

"I can tell what you're thinkin' and there's no need to worry, missy. We're decent, God-fearing people. We'll see that no harm comes to you and we'll do the best we can to get your friend taken care of and back on his feet as well."

"But who? How?" She was still so confused that she

was unable to even come up with a decent question.

"My name's James, James Smith, missy. Our bunch may look a little rough around the edges, but we're just common folks trying to see justice is done. My good friend Alexander knows a little bit about medicine, so your friend is in good hands. But what of yourself, missy? What are you and your friend doing out here alone? Where are you from? You're obviously from a faraway land with the strange manner of dress the two of you exhibit."

Her voice shook a little, although she was trying hard to play it cool. "I'm from ... uh ... Pine Ridge. We were just taking a hike and got lost." Saying they were lost was an understatement. She only wished that lost was all they were.

"I've not heard of that settlement, this Pine Ridge. Is it far away? Is it a fort?"

"Uh, no, just a small town and I have a feeling it's a long, long way from here."

"If we knew of it, we'd surely help you return. Are you hungry? We have some food we can cook over your fire."

"I think I'd like that. Thank you."

The warmth of the fire was a welcome break from what was going on. There were so many emotions bouncing around inside of her that it felt good to just sit there and try to sort things out. Even though their whole world had disappeared, it felt good to be among other people again. The disgust of what the man had tried to do to her wasn't as strong as the concern she was feeling for Joshua. Lying by the fire, she had thought he was dead, and now she watched helplessly from a distance as the man named Alexander was taking care of him. He was weird, for sure, but what would she do in this strange place without him? It appeared that Alexander was trying to pour something into Joshua's mouth. It was a good sign that he was still alive! She unconsciously crossed her fingers in hope. Whatever the liquid was, it brought Joshua back to life, as he began coughing almost as soon as the liquid entered his mouth.

"See, missy? Ol' Alexander knows what he's doin'. Your friend will be fine."

It appeared that Joshua would be okay. At least he was conscious now. Alexander helped Joshua to a sitting position. She could see Joshua slowly moving his head back and forth a little. It was obvious he was in pain, but Alexander had bandaged the wound on his head and cleaned the blood from his face, so he looked a whole lot better than when he was unconscious by the fire. Alexander motioned for another man to come over and the two of them helped Joshua to his feet and brought him over to the fire to sit.

"Joshua, are you okay?" Sheila asked with obvious distress in her voice.

"I think so. I'll let you know when this pounding headache stops. Just what happened here anyway? The last thing I remember was waking up and seeing this ugly face above me."

"That man...that horrible man...we was going to...going to..." Sheila's voice trembled and was trailing off.

"No need to go any further, missy, that little incident is behind us now. He was a bad apple in our little band and we'll take care of 'im proper."

"Who are you guys?" Joshua's brain was clearing enough to realize he had no knowledge of any of the men who were now seated around the campfire.

"Have a bite of this venison, young man, and don't trouble yourself with who we are," James said, cackling with laughter as he spoke, "we're just a traveling band of men trying to make things right. But what of you? It's not normal for us to encounter anyone here in this part of the wilderness. Your manner of dress is like nothing we've seen, so you both must come from some faraway place. The lady said she comes from some village called Pine Ridge. Is that where you be from too?"

Joshua chewed on the bite of venison slowly and stared

into the fire, trying to collect his thoughts. "I'm not sure I know any more."

"We're lost," Sheila blurted out, "we don't know where we are or where we're going."

James got a serious look on his face. "Is this true, young man?'

Joshua hung his head a little. "I'm afraid so. We knew where we were, then something happened. Something strange."

"Strange, ye say?"

"Yes. Everything changed. It's all suddenly different. And now, we've been attacked and we're sitting around a campfire with a bunch of guys dressed up as Indians with faces all covered in black."

James had a serious look come over his face as he considered Joshua's words carefully before answering.

"Have you heard of our little group, then?"

"Believe me, there's no possible way we could've heard of anything or anyone in this place, whatever or wherever we may be."

Again, James carefully considered what he had just heard. He knew all the eyes of his group were upon him, waiting to hear his response and all ready to follow his lead.

"Young man, we're always very careful of the people who are around us. Know this, we are good men, only trying to see that justice is done. There are those out there that do not believe in that justice as we do and would seek to do us harm. But there is something about the two of you that tells me you both believe in the same justice and freedom that we do. You are welcome to stay with us till you get your bearings back and we will stand guard over you both the rest of tonight so you can get a good night's rest. I'm sure the rest will help and that nasty wound on your head will feel much better in the morning."

"And why should we believe you? How do we know you're not like that other bad man?" The tone of Sheila's voice was an obvious mixture of fear and anger.

"You don't know that, lass. You will just have to have faith in us."

"Yes, Sheila, you need to have faith," said Joshua. If looks could kill, Joshua would be dead from the intensity of the evil stare his comment to her brought.

James laughed out loud. "Young man, that is surely a lady of spirit you have traveling with you!"

Joshua blushed a little bit. "Yes, she is something else altogether."

Sheila just cursed a little under her breath, low enough so no one could hear her.

"Zebediah, you and Jeb take first watch. William and Frederick will relieve you. Daniel and I will take the last watch. Alexander, make sure our guests are made as comfortable as possible. A good night's sleep will do us all good."

"Thank you, thank you all so much," said Joshua as Alexander began attending to them. Sheila just stayed by Joshua's side quietly, not knowing what to make of any of what was going on.

6 A FELLOW TRAVELER

An unfamiliar scent filled Sheila's nostrils and brought her out of a deep sleep. After everything that had been going on, she was afraid to open her eyes. It was only after she heard the sound of Joshua's voice that she worked up enough nerve to slowly open them and see what was going on around her. She saw Joshua and Alexander by the campfire and it appeared they were eating.

"Hey there sleepy head! It's about time you woke up. You snore, you know." The playful tone of Joshua's voice made her feel happy and mad at the same time. "Come over here and have something to eat. James has caught us some trout for breakfast!"

"Bite me!" Her reply was less than cordial, but at the same time, it let him know she was okay.

"Do all the people where you're from talk to each other in such a strange manner?" asked James, who was obviously bewildered by their exchange.

"I'm sorry. This is kind of normal for where we come from. I just hope we can get back there somehow," Sheila said wistfully as she got up and joined them by the campfire.

James handed Sheila a piece of trout on a stick they had

cooked over the fire. "Take this and eat, miss, it will help you feel better."

"We'll get back somehow, Sheila. I know we will." Joshua hoped his voice didn't show any of the doubt he had himself about getting back.

"You will be safe traveling with us. We will escort you to the nearest fort and perhaps one of the traders can give you guidance how to get back where you came from."

"I appreciate the offer, James, but I think we'll have to go it on our own."

"Joshua, are you sure? Maybe we should go along with James."

"It sounds tempting Sheila, but I think we should try and retrace our steps. Maybe that will be the key to us getting back."

"I wish I could argue, but this whole thing is just not logical at all. Not even a little bit."

"I know. I'd like to say retracing our steps is a surefire thing, but I really don't have a clue about what's going on. I don't know if it will work."

"You know, buddy boy. I'm just crazy enough to try it your way. What have we got to lose? Something surely has to work in this madness."

"I certainly hope so."

"Well, if you young'uns are set on going your own way, let us help you a little. Our little band liberated some of the King's money yesterday, and you can have some to help you along the way."

"Thanks, James, but we can't take your money. Wait, what did you say? Where did that money come from?"

"Like I told you earlier, we're just out here trying to set things right. The Brits got some money in manners we don't agree with, so we simply liberated it."

"The Brits, did you say?"

"Yes, the Brits."

"This is going to sound funny. But what year is this?"

"You certainly have an air of strangeness about you lad.

It's 1765."

"1765?"

"Yes, lad, 1765."

Joshua and Sheila were dumbstruck by James' statement. They exchanged puzzled glances, but neither of them could muster any words as James produced a small leather bag from the satchel that he had by his side.

"There's a dozen Spanish doubloons here that should be more than enough to get you to where you're going. Please take them."

"James, we appreciate your generosity, but I'm sure you could use this money too."

"Yes, lad, we could use the money. But it makes us feel better to give money the Brits have lost to people that need it more than they do. It appears to me that you two have more of a need for it than they do. I insist you take it. Please."

"Let's take it, Joshua. It might give us the edge we need."

"Well, I guess you're right, Sheila. We really don't know what's ahead, do we?"

"I don't know anything anymore. Nothing. Zilch. Nada. Everything's upside down now."

"Yeah. Only Heaven knows what's in store for us in this place."

The icy look Sheila gave him for mentioning Heaven let Joshua know there was still some fire left in her to enable her to continue this adventure. He wished she was more open to believing, yet a part of him was glad she still had some stubbornness inside her to keep driving him on. With everything that had happened to them since they started the hike, they would probably need all the stubbornness she had to get through this adventure, if they even could survive it.

"It's settled then." James had a satisfied look on his face as he handed Joshua the leather pouch. "You two are the strangest people I have ever run across, what with the way you talk and act, but I have a feeling deep down inside that your journey is just starting. Godspeed."

"Thank you for all your hospitality, James. May you and your gang be blessed in your travels."

"Lad, I believe we will. I believe we will."

Sheila felt nervous twinges inside as she and Joshua left the campsite and headed towards the direction they had come from. This all had to be a dream, yet it felt so real. No way could this be 1765, but even if it was, it had felt good to be among other people, no matter how rough around the edges they seemed to be.

"Sheila, look."

She had been so deep in thought, going over all the events that had just taken place, that the sound of Joshua's voice startled her.

"What? What is it?"

"Look. I think we're near where the tunnel should be. The weird fog is coming back."

"Yes, yes it is. Do you think it will take us back home?"

"I hope so. I really hope so."

7 A LISTENING EAR

"The fog's getting thicker, Joshua. I can't see where I'm going."

"Just keep putting one foot in front of the other and keep going straight. Take my hand to make sure we won't get separated."

The thought of being separated from Joshua was one she hadn't entertained and it terrified her. It was bad enough to be lost in some sort of time warp, but to think of having to do it by herself was more than she wanted to imagine. She wasn't really the hand-holding type, but there was no hesitation as she grabbed ahold of Joshua's hand with a very strong grip.

"Do you think this will get us back home, Joshua?"

"I don't know. I certainly hope so."

The pair walked ahead slowly and carefully, doing their best to keep walking in a straight line.

"Something's changing Joshua. Should we keep going forward?"

"Yeah, I see it too. It's getting darker. But we can't really turn back, because there's nothing here to give us a point of reference to know what turning back would really be."

"I just wish we knew what it would take to..." Sheila's last words trailed off to a whisper. "Joshua, is it..."

"Yes. It is. The fog has suddenly disappeared and we're in pitch darkness. I can't see a thing either."

Sheila gasped. "Do you...do you think we even still exist?"

"Wait. Be quiet and listen."

Sheila stayed as still as she could. "What? What do you hear?"

"Do you hear the echo of your voice?"

"Yes, yes I do."

"Still have your cell phone handy with that flashlight ap?"

"Yes! Yes I do! Why didn't I think of it sooner?" she exclaimed. She hurriedly got out her phone and activated the flashlight ap. The light shone out into the darkness and illuminated a large piece of graffiti. They were in the tunnel again!

"Yes, oh yes, oh yes!" Sheila danced gleefully around Joshua. "We're home! We're home! We're home!"

Joshua didn't have the same euphoric feeling as Sheila. As she took off running towards the end of the tunnel there was something in his spirit that just didn't feel right. She was running so fast, soon all he could see was the light of her phone turning into a speck and leaving him in the darkness. All he could hear was the echo of her footsteps. The strange feeling in his spirit only intensified as he began to follow after her. It was pitch-dark, but he still took off at full speed when he heard her Sheila screaming.

"Sheila, Sheila, are you okay? What is it?" She was trembling all over when he caught up to her.

"Look. Look there."

Joshua looked in the direction she pointed and he immediately knew what had set her off. It was the fog again. It seemed a little brighter, a little soupier, but it was the fog nonetheless.

"Look, Sheila, it probably doesn't mean a thing."

"Doesn't mean a thing? I'll tell you what it means. It means we're still stuck in this...this...oh, I don't even know what this is, but we're still stuck!" It was about the middle of her rant when she quit crying and started uttering profanities as fast as she could.

"Yeah, I know."

"Wait, what?"

"I know. I see the fog too. I'm not too thrilled about it either."

"Well, you certainly don't look too upset about it."

"Believe me, I am upset. But this is still unknown. For all we know, we'll walk through this fog and be right back where we started. I mean, the fog got us into this mess, maybe the fog has to get us out. Right?"

"Or maybe this time, we get to wander around with the dinosaurs." There was no mistaking the sarcasm in her tone of voice. He was amazed at the edge she showed, even with all the fear she was feeling.

"Well, there's only one way to find out. We may as well get started."

"Joshua?"

"Yeah?"

"Uh, would you mind holding my hand? I'm a little scared."

"Sure. I'm scared too."

Both of them felt better as their hands clenched together, the physical bond gave them each the courage to go onward into the thickening fog.

"Can you see anything besides this fog, Joshua?"

"No. No, it's so thick, it's almost like being in the dark, only it's light instead."

"That's an interesting way of looking at it. I'd probably think this was awesome if I weren't so scared. Not only this, but I still can't get that creepy guy back in the woods out of my mind. Him on top of me and seeing you lying there all covered with blood."

"That's behind us now."

60

"Oh, is it? For all we know, we'll be right back with them when we're out of this fog." The string of obscenity that started to flow from her lips made him cringe, yet in a way it was also comforting because it showed she hadn't lost her edge and he had a feeling it was going to take both of them to get through this.

"Can you see it, Sheila? It's getting brighter, isn't it?"

"Yes! I see it too! It is getting brighter!"

"Is that…" Joshua didn't get a chance to finish his question. Sheila let loose of his hand and started walking faster, almost to a run, through the thinning fog to the unmistakable outline of the tunnel entrance, which was growing clearer with each step. Joshua began to run himself, wanting to make sure Sheila didn't get out of his sight. The way things had been going, he didn't even want to think of what might happen if they became separated. Just as that thought entered his mind, he saw her come to a complete halt.

"Look out!" Joshua had just caught up just in time to grab Sheila and drag her out of the way of an oncoming car.

"That was close, I thought you were going to be run over." Joshua looked at Sheila's face and saw a look of terror once again.

"Joshua, look. Just look."

Now that they were safe, Joshua took a chance and looked around at their surroundings for the first time. No forest this time. No old, crumbling turnpike road either. Instead, there was new pavement. Cars were going by, and not just any cars, but old ones. Only they didn't look old. He had seen some of these models before, only they were either old and rusty or restored and shiny. He couldn't even think of words as he watched the cars go by. The reality of being in yet another different time was starting to set in again. He was still in a bit of a daze from the traffic going by when Sheila interrupted his thoughts.

"We're not home. We're not home. We're lost. Lost

61

forever. We're never getting back. Never." Her voice trailed off into silence as she began to cry. Joshua wanted to comfort her, but he was feeling the same things she was. All they could do was kneel at the roadside together as the cars roared by.

Sheila stopped crying and gathered some of her nerve back. "What now, Joshua? What do we do now?"

"I...I don't know."

"What? You always had a plan before and you have nothing? That's not like you at all, Joshua."

"I'm sorry. I've never felt so hopeless before."

"I thought that God of yours always gave you hope." The sneering tone of her voice was quite obvious. Her accusation made Joshua stiffen up.

"You're right, Sheila. He does."

"Well, then, where's this wonderful hope at? What is it going to do for us?" We're who knows where and we're never going to see our home again!"

Joshua carefully considered his words before replying. "Sheila, you may not believe it, but your life has a purpose. My life has a purpose. God has placed us here for a reason, and it's up to us to discover what that purpose is."

"Yay. Purpose. What's that supposed to mean." A few more expletives slipped out of her mouth as she replied.

"I don't know. But if we keep moving on, we'll discover what that purpose is. We'll know it when we know it."

"If I knew I could make it without you, I'd knock you into next week right now."

"That's the whole key. We're in this thing together."

"Yeah. I'm stuck in the past with a nerd-boy. Apparently my 'purpose' in life is to be eternally tortured. Oh wait, you believe in Hell, maybe that's where I'm at."

"No, Sheila, Hell is far, far worse than this."

"Well if it is worse than this, I hope to never find out."

"There is a way to make sure you don't."

"Listen, bub. I've been pretty tolerant of you, but one

more word of preaching in this direction, and I'm going to beat you to a bloody pulp."

"Okay, okay, my lips are sealed." Joshua knew there was a time and a place to share God's plan of salvation, and it was pretty clear this wasn't it.

Joshua stood up and once again looked around. The tunnel was behind them, and a bend in the road hid what was ahead. Meanwhile, the old cars kept buzzing by.

After some careful thought and more than a few words of silent prayer, he got up the nerve to speak, "let's go this way."

Sheila looked tired as she looked up at him and replied, "why?"

"Why not? We can't just sit here. Seeing the tunnel there is a reminder that we're not totally lost. We sort of know where we're at, we just don't know when we're at. I don't think we should go back the way we came just yet. Let's keep moving forward and see what happens."

"That makes no sense. I wish I had a good argument. But I don't. We'll try your way."

Joshua helped her to her feet and they started off walking, both wondering to themselves what might lie ahead. Joshua was still marveling at the antiquity of the cars going by. Even though they were zipping by them, the speeds were much less than what they would be back home. The smells were definitely different too. Whatever they had to face in this time, at least the surroundings were a little more familiar than being back in 1765.

"Look there!" Sheila's words brought him out of his daydreams and alerted him to a car that was up ahead, pulled off to the side of the road. "What do you think we should do?"

"Let's check it out and see why it's pulled over."

"Do you think we should? Do you think it would be safe?"

Joshua laughed. "All those threats back there of beating me up, and you're afraid of whatever's in that car? I think we'll be okay. I don't know what time we're in, but I don't think it's full of serial killers and axe murderers."

"It would only take one," Sheila sneered back at him sarcastically.

As they got closer, Joshua could see the car ahead was even older than the others that were driving by. It looked like one of those old-time types that were in those old silent movies that always got stuck in the ruts in the road or had wheels coming off. It was definitely out of place among all the other cars on the road. It looked like the person that had been driving it was slumped over the wheel.

"Joshua, is that person in there dead?"

"I certainly hope not. Maybe we'll be able to help."

"Eww. You help. I don't want anything to do with old corpses."

"Now, we don't even know what's going on yet. Maybe they're just taking a nap. If they are, we'll just sneak by."

"Yeah, sure. More like the big sleep. Yuck!"

"No. I can definitely see some movement. No corpses for you to deal with."

"Well, that's a relief. Sort of."

As they got closer, Joshua thought he could hear sobs coming from the car in between the sound of the other passing cars. The closer they got, the louder the sobbing became, so there was no mistaking whoever this was, they were not only alive, they definitely also had some sort of problem.

"Now what?" They were standing right next to the car and Sheila was looking to Joshua for direction, but he was uncertain what to do. This was a very old car with no windows, so he couldn't just tap on the window for attention. The driver of the car was a young woman and her distress was so great she didn't even notice their presence, she just kept crying uncontrollably. Joshua looked at Sheila and shrugged his shoulders, a sign to let her know he didn't have a clear plan of action.

"Uh, ma'am?" Joshua leaned into the car a little so the woman could hear him. There was no reaction to him on her part, so he tried again.

"Ma'am, are you okay?" His words were a little louder this time, just in case he wasn't heard the first time. This time, the woman looked up at him. Her eyes were red, swollen and puffy from her tears. All she could do was shake her head and continue crying.

"Just relax and try to take some slow, deep breaths. Is there anything we can do to help?"

This time, she seemed to calm down a little. Joshua couldn't be sure if she was gaining composure or just embarrassed at being caught draining her emotions along the roadside, but that didn't matter to him as long as she was calming down.

"That's the way. Just breathe easy, now. Can you tell us what's wrong and how we can help?"

Sheila was fidgeting around behind Joshua. She was uncomfortable to be around this free-flowing emotional show and didn't really want to be any part of it.

The woman finally regained enough composure to reply to Joshua. "There's nothing you or anyone else can do right now. Just go away. You wouldn't understand."

"Maybe we won't understand your problem at all, but it might help you a little to talk about it and maybe then we would be able to help you out in some small way after all."

"No. It's my problem to deal with and nobody else's. I'm feeling better now, so you can leave me alone and be on your way."

"You seem to have some sort of burden weighing on you. You really don't have to bear all of it on your own, you know."

For the first time, the woman looked and saw that Joshua was not alone and Sheila was there too. Her face seemed to soften a bit seeing the two of them together.

"Is she your girlfriend?"

Sheila was quick to respond to that. "No, I'm not his

girlfriend. We're not even really friends at all, we're just together because..." Her voice trailed off because she really couldn't believe herself what had been happening to the two of them and figured going any further would just convince the woman that she was entirely crazy.

"Well, you're probably better off that way. Relationships are just so much heartbreak."

"Is that why you're so upset? Relationship problems?" asked Joshua softly.

"You could say that. Or lack of a relationship."

"I'm not sure I follow you."

"I really thought I was in love. But then..." the lady just started crying again, unable to finish her sentence.

"Did your boyfriend dump you?" asked Sheila softly.

The woman nodded while still crying.

Joshua gently placed his hand on her shoulder in an attempt to calm her.

"It will be alright. I'm sure you'll be able to meet someone new in time."

"But...but…" The woman broke down, crying hysterically again.

"But what? Get yourself together, girl, it can't be that bad." Sheila's stern voice took the woman by surprise, but it got her attention. The woman turned to look Sheila directly in the eye.

"But I'm pregnant. There. I said it. Are you happy now?"

"So you're pregnant. That's no big deal. Happens all the time." Sheila's casual tone of reply did not go over well.

"No big deal? No big deal? My boyfriend blamed me and left. My friends started talking behind my back and won't be around me anymore. My parents said I couldn't live with them because of the shame. The preacher at my church told me he didn't want me setting a bad example for the younger girls. I have no friends, no family, no money, nothing! I'm on my way to the city to find someone to do an abortion so this would all just go away. I heard there's someone there who will help people like me. I just need to find them."

By the time she finished speaking, the young woman was so worked up she was visibly shaking with a mixture of sorrow and rage. Sheila was speechless after being verbally assaulted with a force she'd never experienced before. Joshua just silently prayed, hoping for some direction and the right words to say to keep the situation from getting worse. It was only a moment till the right words came to him.

"You don't need to go through with this," said Joshua softly.

"Well, I believe that I do. All my troubles go away and I get a fresh start."

"But what about your child?"

"Child? There is no child. At least not yet. Right now it's a blob of tissue, so I need to get it taken care of before it becomes something."

"But God once said before I formed you in the womb, I knew you. Do you think He would say such a thing about a blob of tissue?"

"I think I remember hearing that before. But what does that mean?"

"It's in the Bible. In Jeremiah, if I remember right. It means God knows us, knows who we are and what we're about, even before we're born into this world."

"Well, the way I was treated in my church, I'm not sure God must like me very much anyway."

"Don't judge God by how some misguided people treated you. Those people aren't God. God loves you so much more than you could ever know or imagine."

"Yeah? I have a hard time believing that right now. I mean, where's God at? I'm in trouble and He's nowhere to be found. Just what has He done for me, huh?"

"Well, you might not think this is anything, but I think He led us to you."

The woman and Sheila both shot a curious look at

Joshua.

"What do you mean?" The woman's curiosity was beginning to take her mind off of her plight and make her calmer.

"I mean that I think the only reason we're here right now is because God wants us to be with you right now."

"I'm not sure I understand what you're getting at."

"I can't really explain it. We're not really sure how we came to be here, but I'm starting to believe we are here for a purpose. I think you could possibly be that purpose."

"Me?"

"Or maybe your child."

"Child? I told you, there is no child."

"It may only be this big, but there is a child inside of you." Joshua held his fingers apart with only a small gap to show her what he meant. "It may only be a few weeks, but the child's brain, spinal cord, and heart, are already growing."

"How do you know this stuff? Are you some kind of kid doctor or something?"

The look on the woman's face showed she was obviously puzzled. Joshua knew what he was saying was basic knowledge he had learned in school, but whatever time they were in, it probably wasn't common knowledge just yet. He knew he had to answer carefully.

"I've...uh...read some things and listened to people who have done some extensive research."

"But you've never been in my position, so you don't really know."

"You're right, I don't know exactly what you're going through. But I've known others who have struggled with the same thing you are. I've seen the happiness they've had years later by raising their child. I've seen the pain others have felt later when they've wished their child existed. I've even seen those who had the pain of giving their child up, yet had the satisfaction of knowing they gave the child a chance to live and have a better life with someone else.

And there's one more thing I can share with you. My mother faced the same decision you are facing right now. She got pregnant in high school. My father disappeared and left her alone. It was hard for her, sure, but someone entered her life and helped her deal with it. That someone married her and helped her to raise me. I can't deny that I had a pretty good childhood. Having that kind of a start in life does make me a little biased towards wishing every child would have the same chance of a decent upbringing. And one more thing, my father just recently came back into my life. I don't think anyone is happier than him that I'm still around."

The woman grew quiet. Joshua could tell she was deep in thought, trying to process what he had been telling her.

"I had a lot of good memories of growing up too," she said softly.

"Wouldn't you like your child to have the chance to have the same good memories too? It might be hard to make it happen, but it will be worth it in the end."

"I'm not so sure I agree with you, but I just don't know. I'm so confused. I don't know where to go or what to do. I think I need some time to think this through. And I don't have any money or anyone I can turn to around here. If God had a plan for my child, don't you think he'd make this decision a little easier?"

"Maybe he did. Maybe He sent us here to talk to you."

"What makes you think you being here right now isn't just a coincidence? Coincidences happen all the time. It doesn't mean a thing."

"Trust me on this one. Our being here right now is the furthest thing from a coincidence there could be."

"You said a mouthful there, buddy boy," interjected Sheila, "there's nothing normal about us being here at all."

The woman looked at Sheila, with a puzzled look on her face. "What do you mean by that?"

"Look, lady, there's no way I can explain it to you, because I don't understand it one little bit myself. Even boy genius there has no clue."

The woman was obviously confused, looking back and forth at Joshua and Sheila.

"It almost sounds as if you two are as lost as I am."

"Oh, we're lost alright," said Sheila.

"But," Joshua piped up, "I'm sure it will all work out for us. It has to. I think it will work out for you too. We'll pray for you and the decision you'll be making."

"I'm not trying to insult you, but your prayers aren't going to put much food in my stomach or find me a place to stay."

"About that," said Joshua as he reached into his backpack, "I think these might be a help."

Joshua pulled the doubloons that James had given them out of his backpack.

"Here. We have a dozen of these things, but I think we can spare most of them. I think two of them will be enough for us, you have the rest."

"Are you out of your ever-lovin' mind?" Sheila was obviously upset over Joshua's idea to give away the doubloons.

"Look, Sheila, we don't know if we'll even be able to use these things at all. I have faith that we'll get what we need when we need it."

"Faith? You keep spouting off about that stuff and I'll..." Sheila started spouting obscenities very loudly.

"She's right. I can't accept this money. It's yours and you probably need it. You did say you were lost after all. You may need it to get back home."

"Honestly, I don't know. Maybe we'll need it, maybe we won't. Right now there's no way of knowing if we'll need anything. But one thing we do know is that you have a need. You have a need and we can do something about it. I'm really beginning to believe for sure you're the reason we're here."

Joshua placed the doubloons into the woman's hand and closed his hand around hers to force her to hold them.

"These should be a help. I don't know what they're worth, but they should be worth enough to keep you going for a bit. If you keep going down the road here and get off at the next exit, you should be able to see a church nearby. Go there and find the pastor. Tell him what you've told us and he should be able to help you out."

"Well, I do need a place to stay. Maybe he can help me out with that and with how to get money for these coins. If you're going my way, get in and I'll give you a lift."

"Let's go with her Joshua, I'm getting tired of walking everywhere."

"Sheila, after what we've been going through, I don't think it's time to involve anyone else in our travels."

Sheila looked at Joshua and understood. She absolutely hated what was happening and didn't want any part of what was going on with the two of them to affect anyone else. She didn't like it, but nodded her head in agreement.

"You go on without us. Our trail has to be different. Will you let me pray with you before you go on your way?"

"This whole thing has me confused about what I believe, but what have I got to lose? Okay, go ahead."

"What's your name? It's kind of silly, but we never took the time for introductions. If you haven't figured it out yet, her name's Sheila, and I'm Joshua."

The woman started laughing. "It is funny. I've bared my soul to perfect strangers. I'm happy to meet you Joshua and Sheila. My name is Emily. Emily Swanson."

"Let's pray, Emily."

Joshua knelt and prayed for Emily right beside the car. Sheila was agitated by the whole scene, but was helpless to do anything about it. Nothing that had been happening made a bit of sense to her, this included. Part of her was happy when Joshua ended his prayer, but another part feared what lie ahead now that it seemed this part of the journey was about over.

"Godspeed, Emily. I hope you find the answers you're searching for."

"Thank you for all you've done, Joshua. You and Sheila really helped calm me down. I'm still very confused and scared, but you've given me hope that things will work out, one way or another. I think I'm going to be okay."

"I wish I could say the same for us," said Sheila, her voice betraying her fear.

"I think you two will be fine. Are you sure you won't come with me?"

"No Emily, this is a trip you must make on your own," said Joshua, "and we must make our trip ourselves, whatever it must be."

"Yeah, whatever," muttered Sheila under her breath.

Emily started up her car. "Are you guys really, really sure you won't come along?"

"Yes," said Joshua, "we're sure. Be careful and drive carefully."

"Yeah," added Sheila, "with that old bucket of bolts you're driving, you'd better be real careful."

Emily started her car, waved at the two of them and drove off, leaving the two of them along the road.

"I have to know, where's this church and preacher you sent her to? I don't remember any church near the exit."

"You remember that old cemetery that's near the exit? I think there used to be a church there too."

"But what if you just sent her to an old cemetery? How do you know there's going to be anything else there now?"

"I don't, but I felt it deep down in my spirit to send her there. I remember hearing some of the preachers talking about a really powerful evangelist from around there, too. I hope he's the one she finds."

"Well that's just peachy keen. I'm sure the ghosts and memories will be a big help to her. As for us, what do we do now, prayer-boy? You just sent our ride off into the sunset and gave away most of our money. Shall we look for someone to give our shoes to?" Sheila's sarcastic tone was not the least bit comforting.

"I think our job here is done," replied Joshua. "I think

Emily was the reason God placed us here in this time."

"If God's the one playing games with us, I want to have a word or two with Him."

"You know you can talk to Him any time you want."

Sheila let out a screech. He knew his last comment had hit a nerve.

"Just shut up and quit preaching to me! Let's just keep walking if that's what you want to do."

"Let's turn around and go back towards where we came from. I think that's what we need to do."

"You mean...back to that horrid tunnel?"

"Yes. It seems to be the thing that's tying everything that's happening to us together."

"Yeah. Bad things."

"Maybe this time will be different."

"Yeah. Sure." Sheila wanted to cry, but wouldn't allow herself to appear weaker than Joshua. All she could do was quietly walk alongside Joshua as they headed back toward the tunnel.

8 AN UNLIKELY ALLY

The pair walked silently for a little way before Sheila's curiosity got the best of her.

"Joshua, do you really believe that stuff you were telling Emily?"

"What stuff?"

"That stuff about babies. About giving them a chance in life."

"Absolutely. Life is a precious gift. It should be cherished. Don't you believe that?"

"Well, I don't know. There's lots of times that my life doesn't seem all that special. I've heard lots of different women saying it's their choice what they do with their body, whether they should have babies or not."

"Absolutely. I believe every woman has a choice to decide what they do with their body. I also believe they should be obligated to deal with the results of that decision, as well as the father of the child."

"That's big talk. What would you know about it anyway?"

"It could have been me."

"Huh?" Sheila hadn't expected an answer like that.

"Like I told Emily. It could have been me. I could have

been aborted."

"You're just saying that, right?"

"No. My mom had a tough choice. She was young when she became pregnant. My dad didn't take responsibility and left her alone with that choice. It was very hard for her, but she was brave and decided to keep me. It all worked out, and I'm thankful she had the courage to make that decision every day. I know it doesn't always work out that well for everyone, but I believe everyone deserves that chance to see for themselves."

"Wait a minute, your dad the preacher ran away?"

"No, my step-dad is the preacher. It was my biological dad that ran away. Like I've said before, he's just recently come back into my life. He made a decision to be a Christian and is doing his best to make up for the time we've lost together and for the years he wasted in his own life."

"Ugh. Enough of the Christian talk."

"Okay. No more until you're ready for it."

"Just don't be holding your breath waiting for me to be ready. The time may never come."

"Perhaps. We'll see."

"So what are we going to do if we walk into the tunnel and nothing happens?"

"I honestly don't know. I'm still hoping it will take us back home this time."

"Yeah, you and me both."

The two kept on walking silently back to the tunnel. The old cars continued to pass them by, oblivious to the pair of time travelers they were passing. The opening of the tunnel soon loomed before them. It still looked strange, being all new and shiny instead of old and abandoned, but the newness did make it less of an imposing structure as they were now at the entrance once again.

Joshua turned and looked at Sheila. "Are you ready for this?"

"No. But what choice do we have? We may as well do this."

"Yes, there's no reason to wait around."

The two of them continued onward. A worker who had been outside yelled out to tell them they weren't allowed to go into the tunnel, but they paid him no mind. They knew whatever was to happen was something the worker would have no knowledge of. As the fog started to form again, they also knew he wouldn't be following them either.

"You okay, Sheila?"

"Yes. I'm not afraid this time. What more could this stupid fog do to us that hasn't been done already?"

"Whatever is in store, Jesus will be with us."

"What did I just tell you a little bit ago about that talk?"

"Sorry. But knowing He's with me is how I'm getting through this. You are so much stronger than me, since you're getting through this on your own."

"It's about time you admitted that, buddy boy."

They shared a laugh as the fog was starting to totally envelope them as before. They walked silently through the fog this time, taking measured steps until it started to fade into the darkness of the tunnel.

"Here we are, home, sweet home." Sheila's forced sarcasm was pretty easy to pick up on.

"At least it's not a surprise this time," replied Joshua.

"No, but if we ever get out of this place, I'm never going to sleep without a light again. I've had enough of this complete darkness." Sheila's hand reached out and found Joshua's, neither of them mentioning the need to stick together this time.

"Well, look up ahead. More fog, right on schedule."

"I wish someone would've shared that schedule with me, so I could've avoided this trip altogether." Sheila's voice was sounding tired.

"Let's just hope for the best. No use worrying over what might be." Joshua tried to make his voice sound reassuring.

They entered the fog together silently, walking slowly and carefully. The fog soon becang to fade away, revealing a new destination. They looked around and saw they were once again surrounded by a forest. It was similar to what they'd seen coming out of the tunnel the time they met James, yet the trees were not the same, similar, yet different.

"Joshua, are we... is this..."

"Yes, I think we're back where we met James. But I don't think it's quite the same time. Let's just hope these people are as friendly."

"These people?"

"Yes. Look around. We're not alone."

Sheila looked around and saw what Joshua meant. Indians were appearing from behind what seemed like every tree she could see. Joshua had mentioned hoping they would be friendly, but from where she stood, they looked anything but friendly. She could see painted markings on their faces and bodies and each one seemed to be armed with a bow and arrow, tomahawk, or spear.

"Just be calm, Sheila," Joshua whispered quietly, "if they see we're harmless maybe they'll leave us alone."

"It looks to me like they wouldn't care if we're harmless or not. They look pretty mean. Those terrible things they do in the movies, are they real?"

"I certainly hope not and hope we don't find out the hard way."

The Indians crept closer and closer to them, gradually forming a circle and surrounding the two of them. The menacing look on their faces made them appear very dangerous. They were now close enough that Sheila could hear the sound of their footsteps and their breathing. She became more terrified with each inch they moved closer. Now they were within a few yards of them and getting ever closer. When the Indians drew one step closer, the one that seemed to be leading them let out a war yell right in Joshua's face that was so forceful, Joshua could feel the Indian's spit hitting his face. The sudden sound and the strength behind it made both of them leap in fear. It was an intense fear that only grew deeper when the Indians grabbed them and forced them to walk with them. Their capture brought about war cries from all of the Indian braves, which scared Sheila all the more. She began to cry but did not receive any sympathy from them. Joshua could do nothing as there were too many of them to resist. All they could do was helplessly walk as they were led onward. Their walk was a short one as they soon came to a clearing. In the middle of the clearing was a single post in the ground about seven feet tall. As the leader yelled at them in a language they didn't understand, two of the other Indian braves tied them to the post with what appeared to be strands of animal hide. When the braves were satisfied their prisoners were secure and wouldn't be escaping, they left them alone and went back into the woods.

"What do you think they mean to do with us Joshua?"

"I don't know. It's pretty obvious they're not going to bow down and worship us though."

"How can you crack jokes at a time like this? I mean, really, what is wrong with you?"

"Look, Sheila, I'm every bit as scared as you are, but I still have faith things are going to work out."

"Again with that silly talk. Be thankful we're tied up here, or I'd be pounding on you right now."

"Talking a bit of silly talk there yourself, aren't you?"

Joshua couldn't resist picking on her a little bit. He knew her tough talk was how she was dealing with her fear. The fact of it was he was pretty scared himself and it was only his faith keeping him going. The fear only grew in him when the Indian braves started to return carrying sticks and branches with them. His deepest fears were confirmed when they started to whoop and holler and place the branches around their feet. Their war-like cries was piercing his very soul with fear.

"Joshua, are they going to do what I think they're going to?" Sheila's voice was shaky and breaking up with fear.

Joshua tried to put on a brave front, but his voice betrayed the fear that was within him.

"Yes, I'm afraid they are. They mean to burn us alive!"

Sheila started crying. "I don't want to die, I don't want to die, especially like this. Especially in this place."

"I don't want to die either. But I know where my soul is going if I do die. Do you know where you're going to spend eternity?"

Joshua didn't get a reply. He could hear Sheila openly weeping, obviously terrified by the screaming, dancing Indian braves that surrounded them. He watched in horror as they began to light torches, obviously meant to start the fire, and dance in a circle around them. He had felt there was some sort of purpose for the strange adventure he and Sheila had been on, but there certainly couldn't be any purpose to come from being burned alive. Maybe this was to be the end of their journey. This was the deepest despair he had ever felt in his life, the greatest feeling of hopelessness. He knew now what to do if this was indeed the end of his life. He began to pray.

"Our Father, Who is in Heaven." The words were trailing off in his throat. The Indians had knelt to light the fire around them.

"Hallowed be thy name." He had trouble getting the words out. The branches around his feet had caught fire from the torches and he could see the glee in the eyes of the ones who had started the fire. He could start to feel the heat from the flames.

"Jesus, Help us!"

His cry for help was more like a scream, more forceful than any sound he had ever made before in his entire life. Only a moment had passed after his scream had left his lips when there was an equally forceful scream not very far away. It was some sort of Indian word that he couldn't understand, but it had quite an effect on the braves. Their revelry stopped immediately after the yell as they turned in the direction it had come from. From that direction came, riding on horseback, a fierce-looking brave, one who was dressed a little differently than the rest and seemed to have more importance than the others. Joshua couldn't tell what a single word this brave was saying meant, but the others moved quickly to obey him. They kicked aside the burning branches and worked together to extinguish the flames. The brave keep yelling out orders to the others. Sheila was still crying but Joshua was now intrigued by what was going on around them. The once fierce warriors now appeared to be docile. One of them took out his knife and cut the two of them free. The brave got off of his horse and appeared to be still giving orders to the others. The group of them quietly turned away from them and disappeared back into the trees and left the two of them alone with the Indian brave. Joshua put his arm around Sheila to try and comfort her a little. She was still very upset and it almost appeared if the Indian warrior looked at her with sympathy in his eyes. Joshua couldn't tell what the Indian was doing, but it appeared that he was looking around to see if the others were gone.

"Are you young ones okay?"

Joshua was shocked the Indian spoke to him and even more shocked he spoke English.

"You... you can speak English?"

"Yes. I am Iroquois, but raised by white man."

"But... but... how?"

"Long ago, my family was murdered by another tribe. A white man found me, barely alive, and took me into his home. I grew strong. I learned their ways. When I came of age, I returned to my tribe. Using what I learned from the white man, I became their medicine man. Come. Come walk with me. My medicine hut is nearby. Help the crying one onto my horse. We will go there."

Joshua's mind was numb as he helped Sheila onto the horse. He wasn't sure they should be going anywhere with this mysterious Indian, but he also had no reason to protest. Sheila's face still wore a look of shock and her tears were still flowing, no doubt still overwhelmed by nearly being killed and suddenly saved by this same Indian. He followed along helplessly as the Indian led the horse carrying Sheila along a path through the forest. After nearly being burned alive, his survival instincts were telling him he should be terrified of the savage that was leading them, yet deep down in his spirit, there was a feeling of comfort about this man that he didn't even begin to understand. He only hoped the feeling came from the Spirit, because if it didn't he feared he was going mad. Perhaps there would be answers when they reached his hut. They would soon find out. The medicine hut was now visible through the trees.

"Help the crying one from the horse."

Joshua helped Sheila down from the horse. She seemed to be calming down a little, but there were still some signs of tears flowing down her cheeks. The Indian took the horse and tied it to a small sapling near what appeared to be the entrance to his hut. He then pulled a flap aside, motioned for the two of them to follow, and went inside.

"Joshua, I'm not sure we should be doing this." Sheila's voice was trembling as she spoke.

"I can't think of a single reason why we should. I also can't think of a single reason why we shouldn't. Ever since we set foot in that tunnel, nothing's been the same, nothing's made sense."

Sheila wiped away the tears from her face. "You certainly got that one right."

Joshua pulled back the flap on the hut. "C'mon, let's go."

The two of them entered into the hut. It was dimly lit, with all the light coming from a small fire in the center of the hut. The Indian was already seated by the fire and motioned for them to sit. The two of them sat down on the other side of the fire facing him. They didn't notice the slight smile on his face as they sat.

"Take. Eat."

The Indian passed them each something they weren't familiar with. Joshua bit into it and recognized it as something that resembled jerky as he knew it. Sheila was suspicious of it until she saw Joshua eating his. It had been awhile since she had eaten and was getting hungry.

"My people call me Walking Bear. What are you called?"

"My name is Joshua, and this is Sheila."

"Ah. Joshua, like from the Bible." Joshua was surprised that Walking Bear knew of the Bible, but just nodded silently in response as he took another bite of his food.

"Why are you here? You are not dressed like any whites I have seen and it is unusual to see any here in our forest."

Joshua hesitated. "I'm not really sure how to answer that. We don't really know what we're doing here. We're dressed differently because we're not a part of this place."

"Your answer is strange."

Sheila piped in, "yeah, can't really argue that one. It's very strange."

"I know it's not much of an answer, Walking Bear," said Joshua as he finished his last bite of jerky, "but it's the best we have. In a manner of speaking, we're lost and don't know what we're doing here."

"But seriously, Mr. Bear, why did you save us? Why don't you want to kill us like your friends?" Sheila's question instantly made Joshua very uncomfortable. Walking Bear had been hospitable, but they still didn't know what his intentions towards them were.

Walking Bear motioned toward Joshua. "Because he spoke the name."

"Say what? The name? What name?" Sheila's curiosity was really making Joshua uncomfortable now.

Walking Bear got a serious look on his face. "He spoke the name of Jesus."

Sheila got an annoyed look on her face, rolled her eyes,

and pointed at Joshua. "Great. You're just like him?"

Walking Bear spoke solemnly, "if he knows Jesus, then he is my brother."

"You... you know Jesus?" asked Joshua softly.

"Yes. I learned of Him in the church the white woman who raised me took me to as a child. I learned to know him in my vision quest."

Sheila's curiosity was now aroused. "What's a vision quest?"

"The Vision Quest is a tradition with my people, one that goes back many generations. It is a time for a young brave to be set apart from everyone, to be away from the tribe and to spend prayer and meditation time alone with the Creator. After one leaves on the quest, they are considered dead and return as a new person, a new creation."

Joshua was intrigued by this vision quest, but Sheila didn't seem to be impressed. "I don't see why that is any kind of big deal."

"Big... deal?" Walking Bear seemed confused.

"She means she doesn't understand the importance of your vision quest. Please forgive us for not understanding your ways. Please believe me when I say we do not mean to insult you in any way, we just want to try to understand." Joshua shot Sheila a look to discourage her from any more comments. It didn't have the desired effect.

"I still don't get how just being alone somewhere and praying are... important."

"It is more than that. We are taken blindfolded to a lonely place, so we don't know where we are at. We have no weapons of any kind, no clothing, no food. We remove the blindfold after a period of time and spend time meditating and praying to our Creator."

"You didn't have anything at all?" Sheila was gaining some interest in this story.

"I was given a blanket for warmth, so I wouldn't freeze in the night cold."

"How long does this quest last, Walking Bear?" asked Joshua.

"For some it lasts a number of days, some more, some less. If one is seeking an answer for a specific question, it may end quickly if they get their answer."

"How long did yours last?" asked Sheila.

"They told me it was 40 nights."

"Guess it took a while to get your answer then."

Walking Bear looked solemnly at Sheila. "It took that long for me to submit to the One Above."

"That sounds like a very incredible experience," said Joshua excitedly.

"Others say it was a miracle, but I can say it did change my life. I wanted to quit the first night. I was lonely, hungry, and wanted to go home, back to the tribe. Later I was scared, knowing the wolf was nearby and I had no weapon. I was even more scared and hungry the next day. By the third day, I was getting weak. I was about to give up. It was then that I understood that I was seeking the Spirit to come to me in my own way, not His way. I began to mediate and pray for the One Above to use me in the way he wanted. I don't know how long I prayed this prayer. It seemed like days. Then I heard a voice. A man was there before me. He asked what I was doing. I told him I was asking the Great Spirit to come to me and use me. The man smiled and held out his hands to me. I could see scars on his arms. Then I remembered the stories I had heard in the white man's church about the Holy One nailed to a cross. It was Him."

"You... you saw Jesus?" Joshua was astounded to hear such a thing, but he caught a glimpse of Sheila rolling her eyes.

"Yes. I believe He was the one called Jesus. He gave me food to eat and taught me His way of serving others."

"That is just so incredible." Joshua could hardly believe what he was hearing, an Indian actually having Jesus appear to him.

"There is one more thing he showed me in a vision. Of others I was to serve."

"Others? What others did he mean, Walking Bear, like going to other tribes and sharing the teachings?" Joshua was captivated by this strange story, yet he noticed that Sheila's eyes were wandering around looking at other things.

"I didn't know the meaning of that vision before today. He showed me two people I was to help. Two strangely dressed white people. You."

Sheila had let her attention slip away and was looking around the hut, but from what Walking Bear had just said, she suddenly whirled her head around to look directly at him, her mouth gaping open with surprise. Joshua was speechless.

"It is the will of the One Above for me to serve you. What is it you need?"

"I... I... really don't know where...or how to answer that Walking Bear."

"I understand. You are strange people in a place strange to you. Not sure of your surroundings."

"You said a mouthful there," replied Sheila with a hint of attitude.

"Well, I'm not really sure..." Joshua stopped in mid-sentence as Walking Bear suddenly turned to fix his stare directly at Sheila.

"You. Crying one. You have a need you're not sharing."

"No, I don't think so. I just want to get back to where we came from. I doubt you know the way."

"Your heart is heavy. You try to hide it. You have a pain in your heart for your family. One of them hurts. Is someone sick?"

Sheila felt scared listening to this man who was telling her things she had locked inside.

"My... my sister. She's very sick."

"Tell me more."

"They don't know what is wrong. She keeps getting weaker. Her skin looks strange."

"Is it green like fish in the stream?"

Sheila was getting very uncomfortable having this stranger know so many things in her life.

"Well, I guess you could say it looks like a fish."

"I can help."

"Wait, what? We've seen doctor after doctor after doctor, none of them with a clue and you're suddenly saying you know how to help her right out of the blue?"

"The One Above showed me."

Sheila was speechless. This was getting to be more information than she could process. She looked down at her feet so she wouldn't have to look at either of them as Walking Bear continued.

"Two winters ago, I was praying to the One Above in my lodge on the mountaintop. I did not know why I was there. I just knew I was to be there. I submitted myself to do His will and then my vision came. He showed me blue flowers growing on the mountainside near my lodge. I was to gather the flowers and soak the petals in hot water as a tea. Then my vision showed myself giving the tea to a sick person, one who had the skin that looked like a fish."

Joshua was captivated by the story. "You say you saw all this in a vision?"

"Yes, but not until I fully submitted myself to be obedient."

Sheila was still a little skeptical about the whole thing. "I don't understand why your dream was important."

"It was much more than what you call a dream, crying one. It was direct communication with the One who is above us all."

"Yeah? Well just how do you know that?" Sheila was still not believing this story.

"When Spring came, I went to the spot shown to me on the mountainside. It was covered with the blue flowers from the vision. I gathered up many flowers and kept the petals in my lodge, waiting for a sign of what to do with them."

"So?" The tone of Sheila's voice was edgy to the point of insult. Walking Bear didn't seem to notice.

"Two moons later, a warrior came to me, his eyes fearful, asking for help for his sick daughter. He described the skin I had seen in the vision. I went back with him and saw his daughter, the same person I had seen in the vision. I made the tea, just as I was shown in the vision and gave it to her. She was better after a few days."

"Okay. I'll give you that one. Coincidences do happen now and then." Sheila wasn't letting up one little bit, her expression showing a slight sneer as she spoke.

Walking Bear looked directly into Sheila's eyes as he spoke. "There was one more part of the vision. I was shown two young ones dressed in strange clothes. One of them a crying one. A crying one with a sick sister who needed the blue flowers."

Sheila was silent. She had no answer for that reply. Walking Bear bent down to pick up what appeared to be a small buckskin bag. It had a beaded picture on the front and was tied with what looked like a leather string. He turned and handed the bag to Joshua.

"I have this for you. The One Above showed me that you are the one. The one to bring healing to those with the fish-skin sickness."

"Those? You mean there are more than just Sheila's sister that is sick and we don't know about them?"

"I do not know. I only saw many smiling faces in the vision. The One Above will guide you when it's time. Be obedient and he will show you."

"You're right Walking Bear. Our journey has been, well, different to say the least, but He has been guiding us. We need to stay obedient so we go the right way."

Walking Bear turned to Sheila. "You said you want to get back to where you came from. I cannot take you there, but the vision also showed me how to lead you back to the mist that will take you further on your journey."

Both Sheila and Joshua were shocked. Neither of them had mentioned the fog, yet Walking Bear knew about it from his vision.

"You...you can lead us back?" Sheila's words were much softer now.

"Yes. I know the way back to the mist. I will take you."

"But what of the others? Will we have to go past them again? Do you think they will give us any trouble?" Sheila was still scared from their ordeal of being captured.

"They will follow my orders for now. The tribes are growing restless. There is one called Shingas who is causing trouble nearby. I fear there is much war and shedding of blood soon, but I will trust the One Above to guide me until my time has passed."

Joshua put the pouch containing the flowers into his backpack. "Maybe we should be going, then. You don't need us to be a burden if that Shingas fellow shows up."

"If that is what you wish, we can leave now."

"Are you ready, Sheila?"

"I don't want to spend a minute more in this place than I have to."

"It's settled then. Walking Bear, we're ready to go when you are."

"It will be early in the evening when we get to the place. Are you sure you young ones don't want to sleep and start in the morning?"

"I'm not sure the time of day matters much where we're going, Walking Bear."

"I sense uncertainty in you. But the One Above will not reveal more than you need to know. Trust in Him."

Joshua looked at Walking Bear and nodded silently. He thought back to all the times he became frustrated with how things were going and those times always pointed to his trying to do things his own way, in his own time, instead of waiting on the gentle leading of the Spirit. Whatever time, whatever place this was, the Spirit was still there with them and guiding them. The thought of that was so immense, so humbling.

"Walking Bear, I believe the One Above sent you to us, to say those words. I needed to hear them."

Walking Bear nodded. "I believe that to be true. He is so much more than we can understand."

Sheila turned away from them and muttered under her breath, "you people are so very sick. I don't want any part of this."

"Come," Walking Bear lifted the flap of his hut and motioned for them to follow, "let us be leaving then. Since the crying one is calmed down now, both of you can ride on the horse while I lead."

Sheila shot them both a look of disgust, and it was only the whole uncertainty of the situation that kept her from launching into a string of obscenities as Joshua and Walking Bear helped her up onto the horse behind Joshua. She was really ready to be back in control of what was going on around her.

Walking Bear led the horse quietly along the trail they had followed to get to his hut. Some of the surroundings looked familiar to Joshua, but Sheila had been so upset on the trail the first time she didn't really recognize anything. She did feel uncomfortable though, as if they were being watched. Joshua felt it too. He kept looking around them as the horse walked forward, but didn't see anything or anyone. Occasionally, he thought he caught a glimpse of movement, but there was never anything there.

"I sense your fear, young ones. You are correct to feel it. We are being watched. It is Shingas's warriors that have been following us. But do not fear, for we are under the protection of the One Above."

Sheila whispered nervously, "but how can you know that?"

Walking Bear replied calmly, "because I feel it in my own spirit that my purpose is to get you young ones to your destination."

Joshua understood what Walking Bear meant, but Sheila didn't feel any safer hearing his words. Now she felt like there was an Indian behind every tree, just waiting to jump out and kill them. Her eyes kept darting back and forth nervously as they continued, and she could hear her heart beating in her ears as they approached the spot where the Indians were going to burn them alive. While Sheila was freaking out from the memory, Joshua was saying silent prayers of thanks for being delivered from that fate. It had to be true that God was watching over them, it had to be more than coincidence that Walking Bear had arrived just in time to save them. The memory of the heat from the flames was causing Sheila to shiver as they were approaching what appeared to be the place where they had come out of the fog.

Walking Bear paused, looked around slowly and whispered to Joshua, "there are many around us now. Are we near your destination?"

"I believe we are, Walking Bear. Are we in danger?"

"If the One Above was not protecting our steps, I would say we are."

Walking Bear continued leading the horse slowly. Joshua noticed that he now had a hand on a knife that was on his side. A slight gasp left Sheila's lips and Joshua saw what had caused it. There were Indians now visible on either side of them. They were not close, but they were no longer hiding.

"Walking Bear?"

"Fear not young ones, your destination is before us."

Joshua looked forward, and there it was, the fog was starting to form. As much as Sheila hated seeing it before, this time it was a welcome sight.

"I will go a little further with you young ones before we part."

"Maybe you should come with us Walking Bear. It looks like there might be trouble starting here."

The fog had now fully surrounded them. Nothing from

where they had come from was in view any longer.

"It is not my fate to come with you young ones. My place is with my people."

"Doesn't this fog scare you, Walking Bear?" Sheila was surprised by how calm he remained, even though they were totally wrapped up in the fog, as if it was something normal for him.

"No, crying one. This mist is of the One Above. I know He will do nothing to harm us. This is where we will part."

Walking Bear helped Sheila, then Joshua get off of his horse.

"What will you do now, Walking Bear?" asked Joshua.

"I will go back. My visions have showed me a time of trouble. I must do what the One Above wants me to in that time. Just as you have things He wants you to do. We can do all things through Him."

"Yes!" exclaimed Joshua excitedly, "Philippians 4:13, I can do all things through Christ who strengthens me!"

Sheila rolled her eyes and shook her head.

"It is as you say, young one. We must take our paths. Be safe in the ways of the One Above."

"You too, Walking Bear. I'll pray for your safety."

"And I yours. Farewell Joshua and crying one."

With that, Walking Bear climbed on his horse and started to ride back into the fog from the direction they came.

Sheila watched as the horse carrying Walking Bear disappeared into the fog. "Well, here we go again."

9 MEETING NICHOLAS

"Come on, Sheila. Let's get going."

"What's your hurry? We'll probably just end up in another strange place. Maybe catch up with another of your weird Christian buddies, like the Indian."

"You don't know that. We could be headed home this time. And just what was wrong with Walking Bear? He was a pretty good guy."

"Yeah, just another one of you guys that depend on coincidences and circumstances. Well, I'm getting sick of it. Sick of it, I tell you."

"Just have a little faith."

"Faith? Faith? I'll have your head on a platter you little…" Sheila let loose a string of obscenities in Joshua's direction. This time it was easier to ignore her than usual for some reason. After ranting awhile, Sheila settled down a bit. Either that or she ran out of cuss words to say.

"Feel better now?"

"I probably feel just as good as you do after one of your cute, little prayers."

"That little jab was uncalled for."

"Yeah? Well so's all that preaching at me you've been doing!"

Joshua paused to consider his words before he continued. Had he been too preachy? With everything that had been going on, he really didn't have the time to do much witnessing, it was mostly just relying on his faith to get through each trial that popped up. He knew he had to be gentle with her because this whole adventure was more than enough to break about anyone. It really spoke well about the quality of her inner strength with the way she was handling everything, obscenities not withstanding. The more he considered her point of view, the more he understood it was only his knowledge of God being in control and fully relying on that knowledge that even allowed him to be able to get through these ordeals at all. Getting by without that knowledge showed she was actually so much stronger than him.

"Well, are you going to answer me or just keep staring off into space?"

"I'm sorry, Sheila, I was just thinking. You know, I really admire how strong you've been through all this. I'd never be able to stand up to this without knowing God."

That was something she wasn't expecting to hear. All the crying and behaving badly and he was still giving her a compliment on how strong she was. If he could only see how scared and weak she felt. Every second of this hike seemed a horrible dream, yet it was a dream that kept on going without stopping.

"Yeah, well, you're not too bad to hang out with, you know. That really helps. Kind of geeky, but I've been around worse."

"Well, thanks. I think. Shall we get started then?"

"Yeah, I guess so. I apologize for yelling at you like that. It's just this creepy fog is starting to get to me, you know?"

"I'll let you in on a secret, Sheila. I'm scared to death too. I have to keep reminding myself that God is in control every step of the way. That's what I cling to and what's keeping me going. This whole thing with the fog and tunnel is really worse than any nightmare I've ever had."

"Yeah. Nightmare. That's what I was thinking, too. Anyway, you're right, let's get going. This thing has to end one way or the other. It does, doesn't it?"

"I have faith that it will."

Sheila rolled her eyes in disgust. "Whatever."

They walked onward, deeper into the fog, just as they had before. The slowness of their steps mirrored the uncertainty both of them had. There was no way of knowing what lay ahead. Soon the fog started to fade into darkness until everything was pitch black. Along with the darkness came the familiar sound of water splashing off the floor as it dripped from the ceiling.

"We're here again, aren't we? Back in the tunnel, I mean." The tone of defeat in Sheila's voice was impossible to miss.

"Yeah. We're here again. Maybe this will be the last time."

"Or maybe we're doomed to do this forever."

"Please don't say that. It's like admitting defeat before you even play the game."

"Well, that's how I feel."

"How about we just not talk about it and move along?"

"I'm all for that. If we had lights, you could probably convince me to stay here forever and not bother with whatever's out there."

"Well. No lights. Let's go, Sheila. We may as well find out what's going on the other end of this."

"I guess we have no other choice."

They walked along without saying another word. The continuing slow gait of their footsteps gave away the fact that neither of them was confident they'd find something good at the end of the tunnel. The tunnel was cold as usual, but it was the memory of being nearly burned alive that was putting goose bumps on Sheila's arms. She was definitely ready for all this to be over with, but scared to find out what was ahead of them. Joshua felt a shiver run down his spine as it got lighter and they were surrounded by the fog once again.

"Sheila?" Josh turned and saw her standing there motionless in the shadows.

"Just give me a second, okay?"

He couldn't blame her. Deep down inside, he wasn't in a great hurry to find out what came next either.

"Sure thing. Just take some deep breaths and we'll get to it." He couldn't deny that a few deep breaths would do him some good, too.

"Okay. I'm ready." Sheila started walking ahead on her own.

"You sure?"

"Of course not, you…" Sheila launched into more expletives.

"Well if you put it that way…." Joshua knew better than to try to smooth over her words. She was in a dangerous mood and he thought the best plan of action was to just let it slide. It was really hard to tell which Sheila would be best to travel with this time, the feisty one ready to take on anything and everything, or the broken one he had seen when they were captured by the Indians. Since there was no way of knowing just what might lie ahead, he'd just have to make the most of whatever came their way. He was both amazed and impressed with how she had held up through all they'd gone through. Once again he was reminded that it was only his faith that helped him stand up through everything, yet she had survived it all on her own, relying on her own inner strength. He knew there was no way he could've gotten through any of this on his own.

"Maybe we'll be home this time. Our adventure surely has to end soon, don't you think, Sheila?"

"It had better be. Once you get me safely back home, please promise me that I'll never, ever have to see your face again."

"Let's just take it one step at a time, shall we?" The look on Sheila's face told Joshua that his playful response wasn't received well. They continued walking in silence until light started filtering into the darkness and the appearance of the foggy mist was fully engulfing them once again. Neither of them said a word to the other about the fog this time. With the uncertainty of what lay ahead hanging over both of them, neither of them wanted to get their hopes of returning home too high just yet. They'd been disappointed before and had a feeling disappointment might be ahead again. They walked slowly as the mist started to fade and a familiar form came into view. Sheila saw it first.

"Joshua, do you see what I see?" that was the most excitement Joshua had ever heard in her voice. He thought she saw something that meant their ordeal was over, and he got excited too, until he saw what had gotten her excited. It was the cartoon character graffiti they had seen when their hike first started, yet it wasn't quite the same and she hadn't noticed. The paint was now much older and flaking off. Some of the other graffiti around it wasn't the same as when they started, either.

"Hold up, Sheila, it's not what you think it is."

"Yes! Yes! Yes it is! I remember this! It's the same thing we saw when we first started! We're back!

"No, wait! Get ahold of yourself, it's not the same. Look closer. The paint is much older."

"No. No. No. We're home. We're back. We have to be."

Joshua kept his mouth shut. He knew it was no use to say anything as she stepped closer and inspected the graffiti. He kept his distance and watched as the realization of their dilemma sunk in. Just as he expected, a string of violent obscenities started to pour from her mouth. He thought it best to stand back as she picked up every loose chunk of stone and debris she could find laying around and flung them at the graffiti as hard as she could, all the while keeping the obscenities flowing. After a few minutes, she ran out of things to throw and stood bent over catching her breath, totally drained from her emotional outburst.

"You okay over there?"

"Yeah. I feel better now."

"Really?"

"No, I just thought I'd say that so you'd come closer and I could punch you in the face."

"Well at least you're honest."

Sheila did not appreciate that little bit of bad humor.

"How can you make a joke of all this? You know, I'm really getting sick of being stuck with such a loser like you."

"Hey, I'm frustrated too, but I'm not taking it out on you."

"Ha! No, you just sit around and talk to the sky when you get frustrated. At least I'm dealing with things on my own and being real. You're not living in reality."

"You know I believe it's so much more than that, so much more than just talking to the sky as you say. Everything we do has a purpose. God has a plan for us and wants us to use our skills for His glory."

"Oh, I see. It's God's plan for you to wander aimlessly in an old, wet tunnel for eternity. And your skills are….wait, just what are your skills? I haven't seen anything special from you that's going to save us from this mess, so maybe you have no skills."

Joshua knew it was pointless to continue this conversation. Her mind was set in its' own way and there was no way he was changing it. Nothing was going to change her mind unless she surrendered herself to God.

"Alright. I give up. You win. Let's just get going and see what's out there this time."

"As much as I don't want to go out there, I want even less to stay in here. Getting really tired of this old tunnel. And tired of you, too."

"Fair enough. I don't blame you. It's not been fun for me either, you know."

"Yeah. This couldn't be fun for anyone. And it's beyond me how anyone could trust some sort of god who would allow this to happen to someone."

"I think it will all be clear when all of this is over."

"It's never going to end though, is it?"

"I still believe there's a plan for all of this. I just don't know what it is."

"Well let's get going then. You follow your 'plan' and I'll just take care of myself. Okay?"

"Whatever you want. Let's go."

As they walked out into the daylight, both of them were struck by how familiar everything was. It was almost as if they were back where they belonged, yet not. There were subtle differences everywhere. The pavement was nearly deteriorated into nothing. More rocks from the sides had fallen down. The small crabapple tree by the road was now fully grown. It appeared as if they were in the future.

"Joshua it looks like we're home. Only years in the future, I think. Maybe our families are gone. Maybe everyone's gone."

"I don't know about any of that. But maybe those guys coming this way can tell us something."

Sheila looked in the direction Joshua was pointing and saw what he meant. There was a group of maybe a dozen people in the distance heading in their direction.

"At least it's not Indians this time. I hope these people are a little more friendly. Maybe I'll just stay here with them and let you and that so-called god you talk to keep dancing in and out of this stupid tunnel."

"I know that's just the fear and frustration talking, you don't really mean it."

"Try me."

Joshua let out a long sigh. Just when he thought he was getting her figured out, Sheila would retreat into herself and put a wall up again. There was no use trying to reach her right now, she simply wasn't ready to change, not ready to believe in God, let alone be led by Him. Maybe this time would be different. Maybe the group of people approaching would be able to help and Sheila would be able to see God working through someone else. As the group got closer, Joshua could see they were dressed much like themselves. There was a level of comfort in seeing that, knowing these people may not be very different than themselves. They appeared to be peaceful and smiling. That was comforting, too.

"Hello!" The person that appeared to be the leader of the group called out to them with a hearty wave. The smiles on those with him seemed to be showing a greeting as they drew closer.

"My name is Nicholas. I don't believe I've seen you people around here before."

Sheila's face lit up, probably from the friendliness of the greeting. "My name is Sheila, and this guy with me is named Joshua."

Sheila didn't notice, but the people in the group exchanged glances at the mention of Joshua's name.

Nicholas laughed. "Saying 'guy with me' doesn't sound like a very nice way to introduce a friend."

"Well, he's not a friend, we just ended up on this hike together."

"I see. He isn't quite dressed like you either. So basically, you're not the same kind of people, I take it?"

"Most definitely not! I live for the moment and control what I want to do. He talks up into the air to some imaginary thing he calls God."

"Now Sheila…" Joshua tried to stop her, but Nicholas turned and faced him.

"Your name isn't commonly used much these days. This young lady says you talk to God. Would you say you call yourself a Christian?"

"Yes, yes I would for sure. Jesus Christ is my personal

savior."

Nicholas turned to Sheila. "And are you a Christian, too?"

"No how, no way, not ever! I'm nothing like this fruitcake."

"I see. Joshua, I know someone you need to meet, and we'll take you to her."

Nicholas turned to the people who were in the gang. "Hey everybody! We have a Christian here to take and meet Diana!" The people in the group cheered.

Sheila shook her head and muttered to herself, "more fruitcakes. I'm surrounded by fruitcakes."

Nicholas shook Joshua's hand. "Diana will be so happy to meet you. She's nearby and we'll take you there right away!"

There was something in the friendliness Nicholas was displaying that disturbed Joshua, but he couldn't quite put his finger on what it was. Even with that feeling of dread, he really had little choice other than go along with them.

"Okay, whatever you say. Is that alright with you, Sheila?"

"You bet. Every decision you've made hasn't been good for us. I'm ready for someone else to make some decisions."

"Well, I guess that's settled, then. Lead on Nicholas."

"Sure thing! Just follow me. Diana will be thrilled to meet you."

Nicholas started down a small trail leading off of what was left of the old superhighway. Joshua recognized it as an old access road that he had hiked on once or twice before. Sheila seemed happy to be in the company of people that were very similar to them, but Joshua was getting increasingly uneasy about where all this might lead. He was sure Sheila hadn't noticed, but the group had formed a circle of sorts around them so the two of them were surrounded. He felt like they were almost being herded in the direction the others wanted them to go. At least the surroundings were somewhat familiar. Off to the right, he recognized the remains of an old service building, although it was even more dilapidated than it had been the last time he had passed it. It was only a short distance till they came to a clearing and at the end of the clearing appeared to be a small log cabin.

"Just wait here for a moment, till I make sure things are ready for us."

Nicholas went ahead and talked to two people who looked like they were standing guard outside the door. Joshua felt a shiver run up his spine when they looked in his direction before going inside the cabin. Nicholas was still wearing his cheery smile as he walked back to them.

"When they give us the high sign, it will okay to go in. Just want to make sure everything's okay with Diana so we don't go barging in unexpected."

It was only seconds before yet another person appeared from inside the cabin and motioned for them to come in. The cabin itself was very unassuming and Joshua wondered why anyone of authority would be in such a place. It took his eyes a few moments to adjust to the dimly lit interior of the cabin once they were inside. In the corner of the room, was a business desk, and behind it was a large woman, obviously the one they called Diana.

Nicholas, obviously happy, broke the silence. "Diana, we met these two people up on the trail. This one is called Sheila, and this one is called Joshua."

At the mention of Joshua's name, Diana's facial expression changed from boredom to one of interest.

"Joshua has told us he's a Christian."

Diana leaned forward with a very serious look on her face. "Is that true, Joshua? Are you really a Christian?"

"Yes. Yes, I am."

Joshua's response brought a smile to her lips as she turned her attention to Sheila. "And you, are you a Christian like your friend?"

"He's not my friend, and I'm not like him. No how, no

way."

"Well, that says something for you. Joshua, do you know what your confession of faith means?"

"Yes, it means I get to spend all of eternity with Jesus in Heaven. All because He died on the cross for my sins and gave me His grace.

"Well, that's nice. But that's not what it means. It means you are guilty of illegal practices and you are now a prisoner of the state. Your sentencing will be tomorrow. Take him away gentlemen."

Sheila and Joshua were both stunned as the two guards who had been lurking in the corners of the cabin behind them stepped forward and took ahold of Joshua. He offered no resistance, yet they still handled him roughly as they handcuffed him and half led, half dragged him out the door.

"But. What? I don't understand." Sheila had trouble getting her words out. Her brain just couldn't process what had just happened.

"It's really quite simple," explained Diana, "in our enlightened society it was deemed years ago that Christianity was the source of all of our problems. That is why it was outlawed years ago. You did learn that in school didn't you? It still amazes me that pockets of those outlaws still exist, actually. Just how did you end up in the company of that outlaw? You're not holding something back are you?"

Nicholas spoke up. "Ma'am when we were approaching, it appeared to me as if they were fighting. I saw no signs of them being close to one another or colluding in any way."

"Is this true, Sheila? How did you know this outlaw, Joshua?"

Sheila was shaking with fear and uncertainty. "I've never seen him before today. He's a friend of one of my sister's friends. He just invited me on a hike and…"

"No need to be nervous. We all make the mistake of

being around the wrong people sometimes. It appears to me that is all this is, a mistake. Am I right?"

Sheila couldn't even speak. Words weren't coming to her and this was all happening so fast.

"Nicholas can help you get back home and this whole thing will be over for you. Do you live around here?"

Sheila couldn't tell them of what had been going on during their hike or they'd probably lock her up. She did live nearby, or used to, but she was sure none of her old life existed in whatever time or place this was. She struggled to find words, a plan of action. Finally she came up with something she hoped would work.

"I don't really have a home right now. I'm just passing through." She hoped that would be enough to keep them from asking more questions.

"I see. Nicholas can take you into town and get you a room for the night. You're probably tired and could use a good night's sleep before you head out on your way."

"I don't want to cause you any burden. I can just go on my own way." Part of her thought if they let her go, she could just run back to the tunnel and this mess would all go away.

"Nonsense, it's no trouble at all. The government will reward us quite well for the capture of the criminal, Joshua, so giving you a room for the night can be our way of saying thanks. Maybe after a good night's sleep, you might even want to stick around and watch the execution tomorrow night."

"Execution? What execution?"

"Why, the execution of, Joshua, of course. Surely you know how swift our justice is these days. Practicing Christianity is a crime against the state and carries an immediate death sentence."

"Oh, yeah. I'm sorry, what was I thinking?" Sheila played along and could barely hide her horror at hearing Joshua would be executed.

"Just have a seat outside on the bench. Nicholas will

take you into town where we'll give you a room for the night."

"Okay. Sure. I'd like that." The fact of the matter was that she was completely terrified. Joshua was the one who made all the decisions on this crazy, mixed up journey and now he was gone. Gone, maybe for good from the sound of things. Maybe if she just played along, she would be able to find out what was going on and figure out a way to turn things around. Maybe this would all turn out to just be a big mistake and she and Joshua could get back to the tunnel and get back to where they belonged. It was so confusing to be in a place where people seemed to be so polite, yet the way they treated Joshua was so much the opposite of that. So many thoughts were racing through her mind, it was a relief to see Nicholas coming by to pick her up so there'd be only one thing to concentrate on.

"Climb aboard, young lady, your chariot awaits!"

Sheila was expecting a car ride into town and was quite surprised to see Nicholas coming in a horse and buggy, much like the ones the Mennonites and Amish used back where she came from.

"A buggy ride? I was expecting a ride in a car."

Nicholas laughed out loud. "Surely you know that only government officials are authorized to use motor vehicles for transportation. Diana is the only one around here that can use a car. Where did you say you came from?"

"I didn't say. And never mind about that, it isn't really important. Where are we going?"

"There's a small town nearby that we operate out of in this precinct. I think you'll find it a comfortable place to stay till you get going again."

"What's it called?"

"You don't get out much, do you? You know towns haven't had names in years."

"Ummm...oh, yeah, what was I thinking? I know it's because of...because of..." Sheila was trying her best to bluff her way through this conversation. Things here were obviously very different than the world she left behind.

"Because the old names mostly honored tired, old people or tired, old things. The government is the only thing to be honored now. It's been a much better world now that the government takes care of all our needs. Don't you think so?"

"Yeah. Yeah, sure. You're so right about that." Sheila hoped she was coming off as believable.

"So hard to imagine there are still a few of those crazy Christians out there. Just when you think we've gotten rid of all of them, another one pops up out of nowhere. You should know they'll probably treat you as a celebrity when we get to town for being in the company of a Christian and living to tell the tale."

"The tale?"

"Well, we all know how wicked and evil those Christians are. He was probably going to lead you back to his small tribe and sacrifice you to that so-called God of his. You're so lucky to have escaped that."

"Yeah. That's it. Lucky." This place made no sense to her at all. On the surface, it looked very much like home. The rolling farm fields they passed through as the buggy progressed onward to their destination looked just like the ones near where she lived. It suddenly occurred to her why they looked that way. They were the same fields Joshua and she had driven through on their way to their hiking spot. Things were different though. Now that she had her bearings about their location, the main thing that suddenly stood out was the very proper-looking house that was on top of the hill they were travelling over. It was so perfect before when they drove past, it had looked like a magazine cover. Now it was a burned-out shell of a building, looking like something out of a war zone. This was home, yet not. She also noticed the fields were being tended by small groups of people, with no farm equipment in sight. Things were definitely different now.

"We're almost there," said Nicholas gleefully, in a sing-song voice, "see that house up ahead? That's where you'll be staying tonight. Actually, for as long as you like. Maybe you'll just want to stick around when you see how nice it is here."

"Maybe. We'll see." Sheila got chills from the overly happy looks Nicholas was giving her.

The horse and buggy pulled into the driveway of the house. It looked nice and tranquil, but as soon as the buggy came to a stop, two armed guards, obviously waiting for their arrival, immediately came running out the front door. Not the warm, homey surroundings Sheila had been hoping for. There would be no easy escapes from this place.

"Gentlemen, this is the guest you've been waiting for. See to it she has a nice room, and plenty to eat." Nicholas spoke to the men with a tone of authority. He seemed to have more power here than he let on.

"Now, young lady, the staff here will see to your needs. If there's anything you want, just let them know. I'll be checking in on you later."

"Okay. Thanks." Sheila really didn't have any choice but to be a part of whatever this was. The guards helped her from the buggy and led her to the door. There she was met by a middle-aged woman who was dressed quite plainly.

"Good day, miss. My name is Elsa, and it's my job to attend to your needs while you're staying here with us. What can I get for you?"

"I, uh, well, um, do you have any food?" It hadn't been long since Standing Bear had given her food to eat, but she was hungry for some real food.

"Certainly, ma'am, follow me."

Sheila followed Elsa into the house and down a short hallway to what was obviously the kitchen. Elsa motioned for her to have a seat at a small table and began to open up some cupboards.

"Now then, miss, what can I get for you? What would

you like? Carrots? Potatoes?"

"How about a hamburger?"

Elsa burst into laughter. "That's a good one, miss! You know only government officials can have meat. Do I look like a government official? How about a nice tomato sandwich?"

"I was just joking about the hamburger. The tomato sandwich will be fine."

Sheila was surprised about the hamburger deal, but after learning about the no cars rule, she was able to hide it a little bit easier. The armed guards outside put her on full alert when she came inside the house, so she was already careful to guard her actions.

"So do you take care of people often in this place?" Sheila hoped she might get a little information if she engaged in some light conversation.

"Oh, mostly I just take care of minor officials passing through, or occasional friends of the officials. The really important people stay in a big, fancy hotel in the next town. I guess they're too important to stay in such a small town as this. Anyway, since I take care of the government people, they let me stay here. It's not a bad job. There are several other houses in town that do the same thing. I imagine a few other visitors will be in town to watch the execution tomorrow night."

"Oh yeah, the execution. Tomorrow night you say?"

"Oh yes, justice is swift, and we get them over with as fast as possible. Nothing like a good midnight execution to get the blood pumping, I always say. The more of those Christians we get rid of the better, too! I'm sure you'll be invited to attend the event since you were there during the capture."

"I see. So where is the …uh…criminal being held?"

"Oh, he's just down the road a little piece. They converted the old town post office into a small jail. Don't need much jail space when you get rid of the bad people right away. I don't know why they didn't always do that."

"Um…uh…not that he deserves it, but why isn't there any kind of trial?"

Elsa laughed again. "Oh, sweetie, you can try to hide it all you want, but it's pretty plain to me that you've never been to an execution before. That Christian will get a trial, it usually only takes a few minutes."

"Minutes, eh?"

"Justice being swift is more than just a cliché, dear. It's a way of life. Here's your sandwich. If you want to attend the big show tomorrow night, you should make yourself comfortable and get a good night's sleep. I'll make sure your room is all ready for you."

"Thanks. The sandwich looks good."

The small talk did reveal a lot of details, but it seemed like things were going to happen so fast, there wouldn't be any chance of helping Joshua. And with guards everywhere, there'd be no chance of escape, either. With no possible course of action, she had no choice but to go along with what was going on for the time being. It seemed they were going make sure there wouldn't be any other option for her, either. It couldn't have been a coincidence the moment Elsa left to check on the room that one of the guards passed the window. It also didn't seem like it took more than a moment or two for Elsa to return from having the room ready.

"Your room is ready and waiting for you! I think you'll find it comfortable. Just follow me this way."

Sheila followed Elsa back the same hall that led to the kitchen to the opposite end of the house. The room looked comfortable enough, yet small. She noticed right away that there were no windows in the room, not that it mattered much anyway. If there had been a window, there no doubt would've been a guard right outside of it anyway.

"Just make yourself comfortable here in this nice, little bed and try and get some sleep. Nicholas said he'd be by in the morning to check on you, so I'll let you know when he shows up. Now get yourself some rest!"

Sheila just nodded slowly without saying a word. She sat down on the edge of the bed and looked around the room. There really wasn't much in the room, just a small desk and chair with a couple paintings hanging on the wall. One of the paintings caught her eye and she got up to take a closer look at it. It was a nice, serene forest scene with a small, cozy-looking cottage nestled among the trees. It was so very realistic looking that it was hard to tell she was looking at a painting and not a photograph. She was not sure if it was paranoia or if her eyes were deceiving her, but when she looked at it closely, the light by the door on the cottage appeared to be real. There was no way to be sure, but she had the distinct impression it was really a camera to spy on her. And she was certain that if it was, in fact, a camera then there were probably microphones in there as well. She figured the best thing to do was to just lie down and try to catch a little shuteye. Lying there with her eyes closed she realized there was nothing else she could do. What was happening now was no different than being in a prison. The sound of the knock on the door awoke her with a start. Through the sheer exhaustion of the day, she had fallen asleep without even realizing it.

"Hello, missy, are you asleep in there? There's someone here to see you."

Somehow Sheila knew right away this was the visit Nicholas had promised earlier.

"I'm awake. I'll be right out." At first she thought she'd be escorted from the room, but then realized there was no need for that with her every move being watched and guards outside. She slowly opened the door to the room and walked out towards the entryway of the house. Sure enough, Nicholas was standing there waiting with a big grin on his face.

"I'm sorry to disturb you from your sleep, Sheila, but I have to take care of these appointments when I can. I'm just dropping in to see if you're okay. I also have a few papers for you to sign."

"Papers? What papers?"

"Oh, just a few standard documents stating that you were present during the capture of the criminal and you aren't affiliated with him in any way. You were telling the truth when you said he wasn't your friend, wasn't you?"

Sheila thought about the question before answering. After all they'd been through, it almost seemed cruel to say they weren't friends, but after all, she had never even heard of him before they started on the hike.

"No, we're not friends. We just ended up hiking together somehow."

"Good, good, just write that down in the space right there. Then sign the other one there at the bottom to verify you're not a Christian like the criminal. You're not like him, right?"

"No, I'm definitely not like him."

Sheila filled out the papers, but there was something about doing it that just didn't feel right. The feeling felt really strange, because she wasn't lying about anything, yet it still didn't feel right.

"Now that you've taken care of our paperwork, is there anything we can do for you? Anything we can get you?"

"Could it…would it…I mean…is there any way I could visit Joshua?"

Nicholas pondered the question briefly before answering.

"Well, I don't see why not. I also don't understand why you would want to see him. I mean, you did say you're not a Christian like him, and you don't know him very well at all."

"I…I…I don't really know. Just check on him, I guess. I've gotten to know him a little bit. It just seems a little cold to just up and leave him."

"Yes, yes, I can see that. You seem to be a caring individual, just like the government teaches us to be. I think it would only be right for him to have a visitor before his trial tonight. You are coming to the trial and execution, aren't you? We may want you to make a statement since you were with him when he was captured. It's going to be a great night for it. Very overcast, so there will be no moon or stars. Perfectly dark!"

Sheila felt more than a little uncomfortable at how gleeful Nicholas' voice sounded when he mentioned how dark it would be. An almost ominous tone of joy.

"Well, I guess I could go. I mean, you make it sound like quite an event." The fact of the matter was she really didn't know what else she could do in this strange place yet.

"Great! I'll make sure we have a special spot for you! Elsa will take care of you today, and I'll be back later this evening to pick you up."

"Thanks, that would be great!" Sheila was getting better at putting on a fake smile while her insides were tied in knots.

"Let's get back inside now, Miss Sheila, and I'll fix you some lunch." Elsa took Sheila by the arm to guide her back into the house. Sheila didn't like being guided like this at all.

"Lunch?"

"You must've been really tired, because you slept clear through morning. Now if you'll tell me what you'd like, I have some wonderful vegetables I can use to make a nice lunch salad."

"Just surprise me with what you put in it. It will be fine."

Sheila sat silently at the table as she watched Elsa chopping up the vegetables for the salad. At first, she was surprised there was a knife in the same room as she was, and then she noticed one of the guards lurking at the other end of the hallway. Obviously any attempts of an escape would be immediately met with the "swift justice" she kept hearing about. Elsa soon put the salad down in front of her at the table. It was mostly lettuce with a few small pieces of tomato and carrot with no salad dressing of any kind. Elsa placed a glass of water next to the salad, so evidently there would be no choice of drinks on the menu.

"There you go, Miss Sheila, a salad fit for a king! I hope you like it."

"Oh, I'm sure it's wonderful!" Sheila could barely recognize the sickeningly sweet voice that had just come out of her own mouth. She slowly ate her salad as Elsa stood by and watched. It was more than a little uncomfortable trying to eat while being watched so closely, especially when she noticed the guard was watching as well. It wasn't the best of salads, but she was hungry, so it didn't take long to finish it off.

"Thank you, Elsa, that was a wonderful salad! What do we do now?" There was that sickeningly sweet voice coming out of her mouth again.

"You can read the story of our government! There's a copy of it in the desk drawer back in the bedroom."

"I was hoping for a little more activity than that."

"I'm sorry, but I have strict orders to keep you in the room till Nicholas arrives."

"Well. I guess I should make myself comfortable then." The thought of being held captive like this was disturbing enough to keep the sweet voice from coming out of her mouth this time.

"Yes, the time will pass quickly. You'll see. Let's go get that story set up for you!" Elsa's voice had a sound of excitement to it, but also seemed to be more of an act. As Elsa walked her back the hall, she didn't have to guess, she could hear the footsteps of the guard following them, even though she could tell he was trying to be as quiet as possible. Elsa entered the room first, walking directly to the desk and opening the drawer.

"Here you go! Here's the story of our wonderful government! How it was formed, who the early heroes were, and all the great things it does for us! I don't know about you, but I've read this thing at least a dozen times! It's so inspiring!"

"Oh, I'm sure it is. This will be my first time reading it."

"Wow! Really? You're in for such a treat!"

"I'm sure. Thanks. I appreciate it." Sheila was really starting to have trouble putting on a happy front for these people.

"Well, I'll let you get to your reading. I'll let you know the moment Nicholas is here to pick you up."

"Thanks."

Sheila could hardly wait till the door closed behind Elsa. It was so hard to try being someone else to fool these people, and she feared they were catching on to her fakeness. She sat down at the desk to look at the book Elsa gave her just to pass the time. "The One True World Government" was printed in gold-leaf on the front cover of the book. It reminded her very much of the Gideon Bibles that were in the motel rooms back in their own time. She wasn't really the type who was in to reading much, so she casually flipped through the pages and looked at the pictures. It seemed like each page was filled with images of smiling, happy people. For the first page or so, it seemed like the perfect society, everyone with a smile on their faces. The further she got into the book, though, the more those smiling faces started to seem creepy to the point she had to put the book down and back away from the desk. She couldn't put her finger on it, but there was just something about the pictures that sent chills down her spine that just wouldn't stop. She figured it was best to just lie down on the bed and wait for Nicholas to show up. Several times she drifted off to sleep only to wake up from horrible nightmares of all those smiling faces looking down on her. Nicholas couldn't arrive soon enough. After what seemed like an eternity, Elsa finally came to the door.

"Miss Sheila? Nicholas is here for you."

Sheila rose from the bed. She had a nervous edgy feeling about her that she hoped wasn't too evident as Nicholas greeted her at the door.

"Good evening, Sheila, I hope waiting so long for me wasn't a problem."

"No. No, not at all, it's fine."

"Elsa tells me you were reading the government story. I'm sure that helped the time fly by."

"Oh yes, it was really fascinating." She hoped that lie wasn't as evident as it felt when she said it.

"I'm sure you'll agree it's both educational and inspirational. I've read it many times myself. Now if you're ready, I can take you to see the prisoner. It's just a short walk from here."

"Your jail is really that close?"

"Yes, and if you look down below this house when we leave, you'll see where the trial and execution will take place."

She was really getting unnerved by the happy way these people all talked about an execution. It felt like it was a big event they were looking forward to.

"Okay, I'll try and take notice of it when we leave."

"Oh, don't worry, I'll make sure to point it out for you."

Nicholas looked to Elsa and gave her a silent nod. Elsa nodded in understanding and walked over to the front door and unlocked it. Sheila suddenly realized she had actually been kept prisoner the whole time, even more so than she originally thought. She followed Nicholas outside and, just as she expected would happen by now, the guards she had seen earlier appeared on each side of the house. It made her wonder what the real jail where Joshua was being held was like.

"The jail is just down the road a little piece. We can almost see it from here." Nicholas gestured in the direction they would be heading. "Just a little walk downtown. Let's get going."

Sheila looked around as they began to walk. At least it looked like the guards wouldn't be making the trip with them. They were watching them leave, but not following along. She had been through this town before, yet she didn't really recognize much of anything. It all seemed familiar yet so different. She was still trying to place things in her mind when Nicholas interrupted her thoughts.

"Down there. Down there is where the execution is happening tonight. You can see they're down there setting things up right now."

Sheila looked down where Nicholas was pointing. Now she was starting to remember things a little better. The community park had been down below the hill from the house she had been staying in. She could see a lot of activity going on, but they were too far away for her to be able to tell what the people down there were doing. It was all starting to come together in her memory. Now she understood why things looked a little off as they were walking down the road. Some of the landmarks she had firmly fixed in her mind were now gone. One of the prime memories was of the church. It was a small building, but the steeple rose above all of the other houses near it so it really stood out. What she was seeing now was a vacant lot where it had stood. There was a house next to it where the preacher stayed and it, too, was a vacant lot. There wasn't any sign of anything having been there. Something was sticking in her head about one of the church big wigs living in a big house across the road from the church. At least there was something there instead of just an empty lot, although you couldn't really tell there was a house there. It looked like as some point the house had caught fire and burnt down. All that was left was a big pile of burned up rubble and stone.

"Here we are," Nicholas announced in a sing-song voice, "the local jail, home to your favorite criminal!"

"Jail? I don't remember for sure, but didn't you say this used to be a post office?"

"It was one, once upon a time. When the government did away with the postal service, it was converted to a jail. Came in pretty handy when they first started rounding up those Christians years ago."

"I bet it did." Sheila hoped she was able to hide her shock at Nicholas' comment about rounding up Christians. It really made her wonder what had happened here. With all the bars that were on the doors and windows now, there was little evidence of the old post office, just as there was little evidence of the world she and Joshua had left behind.

"Let's go in, they're expecting us."

Nicholas gave the door two sharp raps, as if it was a code. Immediately the door opened and two guards came out to silently greet them, just as had happened at the house.

"Okay, let's go."

Nicholas held the door open for Sheila to step inside. It was dark inside, the bars on the outside of the building blocked most of the outside light coming in and the only light inside came from a candle burning on the desk.

"Pretty dreary in here."

"It's more than good enough for the criminals that come through here. There aren't that many anyway. The criminal is in the rear cell. Would you like me to come back there with you?"

"No. No thank you, I think I'll be fine."

"Very well. I'll be right here if there's anything you need or he tries something. Just call out and I'll be there in a second. Okay?"

"Thank you. I'll remember that."

Nicholas opened a door up into a room that was even darker than the one they were in. Sheila stepped in slowly and noticed right away that there were no windows at all in this room with the only light coming from a candle on a small shelf on the wall. The room appeared to be a bathroom that had everything removed but the sink and commode and all that was behind bars that had been installed from one wall to the other. There were only a few feet between the back wall and the bars and it was obvious

116

it wasn't constructed to allow for many visitors. Through the shadows Sheila recognized the kneeling form of Joshua in the rear corner of the cell.

"Joshua?"

The kneeling figure got up slowly and awkwardly and turned to face the front of the cell.

"Sheila?"

"Yeah, it's me. How are you doing?"

"Other than being beat around, I'm okay."

"They hit you?"

"Yeah, I took some abuse. But nothing that compares with what Jesus went through for us."

"Listen, dude. Maybe you should get off this Jesus kick. Because of Him, they're going to kill you, you know."

"Yeah. I know. I always knew I might have to die for my faith someday. I just didn't think it would ever be a strange place like this. Not this way."

"Get it together here! This is your life we're talking about! Just tell them you were kidding about all this Christian stuff, and maybe they'll let you go."

"Christ died for me. How could I ever deny Him, knowing that?"

"I don't get you. I don't get this! You're putting your life on the line for some stupid, old book!"

"But it's real. I believe it is. I know it is. If I have to give my life for Him, so be it. I know where I'll be spending eternity."

"They want me to be there tonight. They want me to be a part of it. I can't do anything to save you."

"I don't expect you to do anything, Sheila. You don't have to watch. You're free to go on without me. Maybe the tunnel will take you back to where you belong."

"I don't know what to do. You were the one with the plan."

"Listen. When I tried to do things the way I thought they should be I failed. When I prayed and sought an answer from Jesus…well…it wasn't always what I wanted, but it always worked out to glorify God somehow, some way. I was praying for you when you showed up. Jesus has a plan for your life if you let Him show you the way."

"You're going to die tonight. You're going to die and you're telling me there's some sort of plan that this is all a part of?"

"Somehow, yes it is, even though I don't see it or understand it. Maybe I do die tonight. Somehow God is going to use it for his plan."

"Well, the only purpose I see coming from this is if they throw your dead body on a compost pile and you become fertilizer for the plants. Is that what you want to be? Plant food? Food for the worms?"

"If it's God's will, so be it."

"You…you…" Sheila was so frustrated no more words will come out.

"It's okay. You don't have to understand it now. Just think about everything that's happened to us and maybe someday you'll feel the need to seek salvation."

"I give up! You're hopeless!"

Sheila stormed out the door mumbling all sorts of obscenities, right past a widely grinning Nicholas who had been eavesdropping the whole time. Everything was going exactly as he had hoped. What made him the happiest was that now there was no doubt his execution would be taking place without a hitch. He had a feeling the girl might try and talk the prisoner into changing his story and nothing thrilled him more than hearing his prisoner was sticking with his illegal beliefs. This ensured there'd be a successful execution and news of it would spread far and wide. A successful execution gave him a good shot at getting a cushy government job, something he'd been after all along.

10 THE BIG EVENT

Sheila paced around the room for hours after she was escorted back to the house. She just couldn't understand how Joshua could be so stubborn about not changing his story to save his own life. Even if he really believed everything he said, what would the harm be in just lying about it? She, herself, would say just about anything to escape such a fate. It just didn't add up. The sun had been down for some time now. There was no clock in her room, so she didn't know what time it was, how much time was left till the execution. Just the thought of it made her shudder. She hadn't known Joshua long, but he'd always been there for her every step of the way in this horrible journey they'd been on. Just then, a knock came on the door.

"Hello in there. Are you awake?" It had been a long day, yet Elsa's voice sounded strangely energized.

"Yes, yes I am." Sheila was exhausted, but she tried to project the same kind of energy in her voice.

"Nicholas is here to escort you to the big event!"

The excitement in Elsa's voice gave Sheila a sick feeling in her stomach. She slowly opened the door to see their smiling faces. She tried to smile back at them, hoping they couldn't detect how fake her smile really was. Her survival instincts were telling her it was best they thought she was on their side for now. That seemed to be the best course of action till she could figure some things out.

"I have a chariot waiting outside for you Miss Sheila, ready to take you to the big show! I took the liberty of reserving you a special seat up front so you can be in the center of the action!"

"Thanks." Sheila was really having trouble acting enthused about all this.

"Follow me, we don't want to be late now, do we? Everything should be set up and waiting for our arrival."

Sheila silently followed Nicholas out of the house. The guards were every bit as noticeable, but this time they seemed more relaxed. Out in front was a horse-drawn buggy, but this one was much fancier than the one that had brought her here. There was also a driver for this one. As she climbed up into the buggy she could see the area down below where they had earlier been getting things set up for the execution. If she didn't know better, she'd swear it was lit up for a carnival. As they began the short ride down to the execution site, Nicholas tried to make small talk, but all she could do was nod silently. The whole thing seemed so surreal. Maybe she had been in some sort of accident and all the different places the tunnel took them to were just a figment of her imagination and she was really laying in a coma in a hospital someplace. Or maybe one of those idiots she hung out with slipped her some drugs and this was a bad drug experience. That would make much more sense than anything. Yet it was all so real. Too real to be a fantasy. As they made a turn past the post office turned jail, she began to notice people walking along the road on their way to the execution. Everyone seemed like they were happy and going to a party. She couldn't quite grasp how people could feel such a way. She didn't know how or why, but suddenly life was becoming more of a precious thing in her eyes. The whole sugary-sweet atmosphere of this stupid, little town was really starting to sicken her, especially the way they all talked of executions as being a good thing. The whole trip was only a few minutes, but it seemed to drag on so very much longer. She hadn't felt it before, but their arrival brought a feeling of dread to her whole being like she had never felt before. The happy, joyous expressions of the people coming to greet them wasn't helping with that either.

"Nicholas, so good to see you! I assume the lovely lady with you is our esteemed guest?"

The rotund man greeting Nicholas reminded Sheila of a ringmaster at a circus the way he was dressed. Fitting, since this seemed to be some sort of circus atmosphere.

"Yes, Thomas, this is Sheila, the one I told you about. She's the one who was with the criminal when we captured him."

"Oh Nicholas, this will be sure to get you the recognition you deserve! I hope you remember us little people when you reach the top."

"Never you worry, Thomas, I'll be sure to take care of those who took care of me. Is everything all set up? Everything in place?"

"Oh yes, I have my table set up where I'll judge from. Your portable desk is set up right beside the criminal's cage, and I have a seat for the lovely Miss Sheila right across from you. It's all perfectly situated for everyone to have a good view of the proceedings. And a good view of the machines, of course. Mustn't forget the machines!"

"Of course not! They are the whole show, after all. I knew I could count on you to get it all set up just right."

"Thank you for your confidence, Nicholas! Now if you folks will just get seated, it's almost midnight, and we mustn't get started late, you know."

"No, we mustn't be late. Let's get seated, Sheila, we don't want to keep the crowd waiting."

Sheila nodded and followed Thomas to the seat he had set up for her. The whole area around them was lit up with portable lights which gave the surroundings an odd feel since it was pitch black wherever the light didn't reach. As Nicholas was leading her to where they were going to have her sit, she could see the table where Thomas would be sitting to act as judge. It was a small table, but it was heavily decorated in gold trim with a lot of fancy designs. Next to it was a similarly decorated podium, where she imagined Nicholas would be. She knew her suspicions were correct as Nicholas motioned for her to sit on a seat across from the podium. As she was sitting down, her eyes caught sight of the cage Thomas had mentioned. The lighting was arranged so that none of it would illuminate the cage, but she could already tell that the figure in the shadows of the cage was Joshua. And what of the machines they mentioned? There were three large objects in front of them covered with what looked like shiny, satin sheets. She guessed the machines they referred to must be under the sheets. Thomas was seated behind his table and now Nicholas had taken his place behind his podium.

"Alright, ladies, gentlemen, and folks of all other persuasions, the time for the big show is here!" exclaimed Thomas. "Because of the quick thinking of our own Nicholas, a Christian has been captured and will soon realize the swift judgment of our fair government! Our little town will be famous and spoken of for many miles around!"

Sheila was getting a sick feeling in her stomach as the crowd started to cheer and applaud.

Thomas continued. "Let's get right to it folks and start with the facts in this case. Nicholas, isn't it true the subject admitted to you he was a Christian?"

Nicholas stood as perfectly straight as he could and proudly proclaimed loudly so all in attendance could hear him plainly, "yes, sir, that is in fact, the very truth."

"And were there witnesses to that effect?"

"Yes, sir, all the members of my patrol were there for the confession."

"Excellent. Now for article number two."

Sheila watched as Thomas pulled out Joshua's backpack out from behind his judge's table.

"Here within this backpack is," Thomas paused for suspense, "illegal and banned contraband!"

Sheila started to fidget in her chair as she saw Thomas pull Joshua's Bible out of the backpack and hold it up high for all to see. She could hear the crowd murmuring all around her as they recognized what he was holding up.

"There is no other choice when faced with these facts except to sentence the criminal to death!"

As soon as Thomas uttered the last words, bright spotlights shined on Joshua. Sheila could tell they were meant to be blinding and intimidating by the stance Joshua took in the cage.

"Do you, the convicted criminal, have any last statements or arguments? Do you wish to denounce your alleged faith and beg our court for leniency?"

Joshua looked tired, beaten. He slowly raised his head to face Thomas before he spoke loudly. "No sir. Jesus Christ is my Lord and Savior and I will NOT deny Him. If it means I die for Him, so be it. It will only be because He allows it."

Thomas' face turned a bright red as he screamed out, "prepare the machines! Let us rid our town of this virus and make it pure again! Gentlemen…the machines!"

Three men stepped forward and removed the sheets covering the machines. It was obvious they had been practicing the ceremony, because their actions were very coordinated. A feeling of pain and anguish shot right through Sheila when she saw what they were calling machines. Beneath the sheets were three shiny, highly-polished guillotines. Two guards opened the door to Joshua's cage. Sheila was amazed how calm Joshua looked, how he didn't struggle with the guards and appeared willing to accept his fate. The guards exchanged perplexed glances, their plans of staging a show of roughing up a struggling prisoner shattered by this compliant young man. Sheila could see Joshua smiling and saying something quietly to the guards, something that really seemed to make the guards uneasy. She imagined he was probably doing that preaching thing like usual. When they reached the guillotine, Joshua didn't even wait for the guards to get him into position. Instead, he kneeled down himself, voluntarily placing his head into the bottom groove of the machine. The guards were so shocked at his behavior, they paused a moment before tying his hands behind his back and placing the basket to catch his head underneath him. It was not only obvious the guards were unsettled by Joshua's behavior, but the crowd was starting to murmur among themselves as well. Thomas was beginning to get nervous. This was to be a grand spectacle to draw attention to himself and Nicholas. Instead, this criminal appeared to be gaining sympathy with the crowd. He decided this would not do. This would not do at all.

"Ladies and gentlemen! I would like to introduce you all to a young lady named Sheila. She was with the criminal when he was captured. It's not often we have a special guest to confirm the guilt of the accused. Miss Sheila, can you confirm the criminal, Joshua, did in fact partake in Christian activity?"

Sheila looked at Joshua. Tears started to form in her eyes and roll down her cheeks as she saw the calmness in his eyes.

"Sheila!" Joshua called out to her. "Just tell the truth. No matter what you say, I won't hold anything against you. It will be alright. I'm in God's hands. Just tell the truth."

Sheila looked down at her feet, trying to decide what to do. Then the answer came to her.

"Yes. Yes, Joshua did act like a Christian. No wait, I didn't mean he acts like a Christian, I mean he lives like a Christian through his actions. He always thinks of others. He always tries to help others and put them first. He always talks to Jesus and told me how Jesus helps him.

From everything I've been seeing here today, I don't think that's too bad of a thing."

Thomas was getting agitated. "Just what exactly are you saying?"

"I'm saying, if what Joshua has done is wrong, then I don't want to be on the side of right. I want to be a criminal too. I guess what I'm saying is, I'd rather be a Christian than be like you people."

"Be careful with your words, young lady, you don't know what you're saying."

Sheila was getting louder. "Oh, I do know what I'm saying. I'm saying Joshua wouldn't be so willing to put his life on the line if Jesus wasn't real. He wouldn't be willing to die for nothing. Because of his belief, I believe now too. I believe in Jesus as the Son of God and I believe He died on the cross for me!"

Sheila looked at Joshua, but spoke loudly enough for the whole crowd to hear. "Thank you for teaching me the truth!"

Thomas was beside himself in anger. "Seize her! Seize her now! That was a public confession! We don't need a trial!"

Sheila tried to be brave like Joshua when the guards grabbed her. She struggled a little by sheer instinct, and she was scared to death, but she still maintained her composure as the guards placed her on the second guillotine next to Joshua.

"Sheila, that was awesome!" The size of the smile on Joshua's face gave no indication his life would soon be over. "You won't regret your decision. When Jesus was crucified, he told the thief on the cross next to him that he'd be with him in Heaven. That will be the same for you. When these blades drop, we'll be with Jesus in Heaven."

Sheila managed a feeble smile. "We better be. I bet my life on it because of you."

Thomas had seen enough. The show wasn't turning out like he planned at all. "The time has come to bring the rein of these criminals to an end!"

The crowd was hushed. This show was not at all what they had expected. Suddenly, a series of loud explosions behind them took their attention.

"Three!" The loud cry thundered through the air. Almost as in an answer to the call, the lights went out, leaving everything in pitch darkness.

"Three!" This time the cry came from a different direction. There were more explosions going off in a different location.

"Guards! Guards!" Thomas and Nicholas were both screaming for the guards, but the guards were not responding. No one could see what was going on, with the only light source being that of the explosions.

"Three!" The people in the crowd were getting scared and disoriented with the darkness and explosions.

"Three!" Joshua and Sheila, just like the crowd, wondered what was happening. Just then, a whisper came out of the darkness.

"I'm a friend. Stay quiet and we'll get you out of here."

Joshua felt strong arms lifting him up from the guillotine. Whoever those strong arms belonged to, threw him over their shoulder like a big sack of potatoes and started to run away from the confusion behind them. By the sound of the footsteps, he guessed that someone else had Sheila.

"Three!" Another cry and more explosions. This time he could tell they were getting some distance from the guillotines.

"Three!" The cries and explosions were getting further behind them. Joshua sensed they were moving through the forest that was behind the place where the trial had been, but he had no way of knowing for sure. He was amazed at how well whoever was carrying him navigated so well in the darkness. They obviously had to know where they were going and had to be pretty powerful to carry someone his size so easily.

"Three?" This time the call was quiet, the sound of a very loud whisper. Joshua's benefactor quickly headed in the direction the voice came from.

"We clear?"

"Yes. This way. We have Tunnel Zoe ready."

Joshua still couldn't see anything going on, but there were lots of swishing noises going on and the creaking of wood. With the unidentified person mentioning a tunnel, Joshua supposed the people may be covering up the tracks leading to a secret tunnel entrance. His benefactor sat him down on a cold, rough surface which would be very much like the floor of a tunnel or cave. His ears were telling him from the sounds of breathing next to him that Sheila was there too.

"I think we're covered now."

"Are the watchers in place?"

"Yes, they're watching for anyone who could've followed you."

"And the rest of the party?"

"From our reports so far, everyone is accounted for. No losses."

"Excellent! The Spirit has been with us yet again!"

"Should we shed light on our guests now?"

"Yes, everything appears to be under control. I will go on up ahead to our meeting area."

Joshua could hear the sound of a match striking and soon the light from a lantern was illuminating the area around them. It looked as if they were in some kind of cave underground. Sheila appeared to be okay but looked pretty scared.

"What is this place?"

"This is an old coal mining tunnel. We use them quite often in our raids, some of us who are too well known to the government live down here. My name is Elias, by the way, but you can call me Eli. Let me get you and your friend untied. We must get going down to the meeting area to figure out our next move."

"I'm Joshua, and this is Sheila"

"Pleased to meet you. We must get going. We don't like to stay too close to the entrances of our tunnels if we can help it."

Eli quickly untied Joshua first and then Sheila. It hurt at first to stand up, but they soon stretched enough to be ready to keep up with Eli as he led them down the passageway. At times they had to stoop over because the ceiling was so low. Sheila brushed against the walls several times when the passageway narrowed but she never complained.

"Eli, what exactly is going on here?" Sheila had thought the words, but Joshua was brave enough to speak them.

"The first thing, you must meet our leader, he's the one that came up with the plan to free you."

"The big guy?"

"Yes. He's quite a mastermind when it comes to planning our raids."

"Raids? Are you like pirates or what?"

Eli laughed out loud at being called a pirate. "No. No, we're not pirates. We're criminals like yourself."

"Criminals?"

"Yes. Criminals. Believers in the Lord in direct defiance of the government. We have not given up the fight to spread the Word."

"Wow." Joshua was so overwhelmed he couldn't say any more.

It seemed like they had walked through the mining tunnel for miles when they saw a brighter light up ahead. This was where Eli was leading them. Eli put the lantern out when they got close enough for the light ahead to provide enough light for them to see where they were going. Once they got there, Joshua could see the passageway opened up into a much larger room. There wasn't a lot of furniture in the room, but it was brightly lit with multiple lanterns and actually seemed a bit cozy. The next thing Joshua noticed was a huge man sitting at a desk at the far side of the room.

"Sir, our guests are here. Joshua and Sheila, I'd like you to meet our leader."

11 A STRANGE REUNION

The big man got up from his desk and rose to greet them. His eyes met Joshua's and at that instance, both their mouths dropped open with shock. Eli and Sheila were both taken by surprise at the spectacle of the two staring at each other.

"Sir, what is wrong?" Eli had been with his leader for many raids, and had never seen him so stunned before.

The big man could not take his eyes off of Joshua. His wonder was so intense he didn't even hear Eli's question.

"I…know…you. I know…who you are." The big man's words could barely come out.

Joshua was finding it equally hard to speak. "I don't know you. But you look very much like someone I do know."

Eli was dumbfounded by what was going on in front of him. "Three, just what is going on here?"

The big man turned to Eli. "I know him. This is Joshua Carson."

Joshua was stunned. They were in a strange place, a land and time they did not know, and yet this person knew him. "And you are?"

The big man stuck out his hand. "My name's Jim. Jim Dunning."

Eli piped in and interrupted. "Jim Dunning the Third.

You probably heard us shouting 'Three' during the raid. That's our signal to him. We like to call him JD3 for short."

Joshua was even more stunned. So stunned he couldn't speak. Sheila didn't know what was going on and wasn't afraid to ask.

"Joshua, just what is going on here? How does this man know you?"

Joshua, still very stunned, stood silently for a moment, shaking his head and thinking over everything that had just happened. It was so incredible, so hard to believe, but it had to be true.

"Sheila. He knows me because Jim Dunning is my father. Which means he is my father's grandson. And I guess that makes me his great uncle."

"You're kidding, right?"

"I couldn't kid about something this crazy. This is all making my head spin."

"You really are Joshua Carson, aren't you?" Jim still wore the same look of astonishment that Joshua did.

"Well, yes. Yes, I am. You know, you really look so very much like my father."

"I'm happy and proud to hear you say that. You know, I never got to meet him. It's got to be some sort of miracle you're here now. You disappeared so many years ago. My dad told me all about it happening before he was born."

"How did you know it was me?"

Jim went over to the desk and brought back a picture. "Because of this. And the stories my father used to tell."

Joshua looked at the picture Jim had handed him. It was a picture of him with his father, step-father, uncle, and grandfather all on the front porch of the house back at Brooksville. The picture wasn't that old to him, but by the condition of the print, he could tell it had been around for many years.

"I remember this picture. We had a good time working on the house that day. A good time in prayer, too."

"It's an obvious miracle you're standing here before me, but what is really going on here? You're still young, like in the picture, and you should be so very old by now."

"It's hard to explain. In fact, I don't think I can, because I really don't understand it myself. I just know God has led us the whole way."

"He was definitely with us tonight. I thought it would be a risky rescue, but when your friend here made a proclamation of faith and joined you, I had a feeling we might need a miracle to get you both out. As it turned out, it couldn't have gone smoother. Everyone made it back in one piece with no problem, too. A good night for all of us! It still doesn't explain how or why you're here now, though."

"It's that tunnel! That stupid tunnel! Every time we step into it something weird happens!" Everyone turned and looked at Sheila, surprised by her outburst.

"Everything was fine before we went on that stupid hike and went into that stupid tunnel!"

"A tunnel? Like the ones we travel in here? Tell us more about it." Jim was obviously intrigued by the mention of the tunnel.

"Um. Well. We went into the tunnel, the tunnel at the old super highway, and came out in other places. Every time we go in, we come out in another time and place."

Joshua suddenly looked like he had a revelation. "I just had a thought, Sheila. If what happened to us through the tunnel never took place, would you have ever made the faith decision you just did back there at the machines? Think about it."

"What are you trying to say, Joshua?"

"I'm saying that maybe the tunnel is part of God's plan to bring you to Him. If so, it worked, didn't it?"

"Yeah, I guess so. I wish he would've chosen a more painless path than this one."

Eli interrupted. "Three, are you buying this story? Sounds pretty suspicious to me."

"The Lord works in mysterious ways, Eli. We all know that. What can be more mysterious than my long-lost great uncle showing up all these years later? Without having aged, to boot. No, I don't believe this is an elaborate hoax, but one of God's miracles. And a magnificent miracle at that."

"Eli, if my backpack were here, I could show you another picture of my father and see just how much the Jim Dunning before you looks like him. Maybe that would help you believe."

Eli still looked a big suspicious and took a step backwards as if he was getting ready for escape.

"Looking for this, uncle?" Jim laughed as he produced Joshua's backpack from beside the desk. "When I saw them pull your Bible out of here for evidence, I thought it would be important enough to grab it along with you."

"Wow! I thought it would be gone forever!" Joshua took his backpack from Jim and started going through it.

"I hope what you're after is in there. I'd like to see that picture whether we make Eli a believer or not."

"Looks like everything is still in here. I'm glad they left my Bible intact, because that's where the picture is at. Right here at Romans 5:8"

"While we were still sinners, Christ died for us!" Jim and Eli both spouted out the verse like they had been rehearsing it for this very moment.

"Well, it's nice to know you guys are familiar with the verse," laughed Joshua. "Even nicer that the picture is still here!"

"Yes!" Jim pumped his fist with excitement.

"Here you go." Joshua handed the picture to Jim, and Eli peeked at it over his shoulder. The two men were obviously amazed at what they were looking at. Eli finally broke the silence.

"I'd swear this was a picture of you, Three. I don't recognize any of those other faces though, except for the kid."

Jim looked up at Joshua. "So this is my grandfather? What was he like? Can you tell me about him? I mean, my father told me a few stories, but you were there at the beginning, you have to know something more."

"When he came into my life, he was a pretty scary man at first, but when he found the Lord, he became a changed man. Really had a heart of gold and really dove into the Bible to learn all he could. When he witnessed to you, you had better listen, if you knew what was good for you."

Eli started laughing. "Sounds like someone I know. Funny how a personality like that can sneak down through the family tree!"

Jim walked over to a door on the other side of the room. "Joshua, I have something here you might recognize." Jim disappeared behind the door and soon appeared again, pushing a motorcycle.

"It's his bike!" Joshua could not contain his excitement and ran over for a closer look.

"Yes, that's definitely it! Obviously much older now, but it's the same bike. I helped him when he made this new roll bar and watched as he painted this cross on the gas tank."

"I tried to take care of it as best I could, sort of a memento of my ancestors. I wish I could've known him."

"So he was gone before you were born?"

"Yes. It was during the time of trouble, from what my dad told me. Dad was the one that found the bike afterward."

"Afterward?"

"Yeah. No one ever knew what happened to him, though. Dad was young when the government came to round up the Christians. He told me that granddad stayed behind to try and give everyone else time to get away. Dad said it was this sacrifice that allowed them all to escape. Different people went back secretly to recover as much of their stuff as they could from the town. The bike was all we ever found of granddad, though. Dad thought he may have escaped into the mountains and fought on by himself. He figured if they had gotten him, the government would have put him on display as an example. It's really hard to tell with no evidence."

"That would've been very much like him to do that. I never knew of anyone that could stop him when he put his mind towards something."

"From what dad told me, losing you stopped him for a little bit."

"What?"

"He was devastated for a while when you disappeared. He told dad he couldn't go on until one day, the Holy Spirit told him you were okay. He never understood it, but had a peace about it. And now I see before me the Holy Spirit wasn't lying, you are alright after all."

"It really hit him that hard?"

"Dad told me he searched for almost a week non-stop without eating or sleeping. Your uncle and grandfather were out searching most of the time, too. That's them in the picture with you, isn't it?"

"Yes, that's them. My grandfather, your great-grandfather, was so full of wisdom. Just as home in a city as living off the land in the mountains. My uncle, well he and my father were like two peas in a pod. They grew up close as friends when they were kids and somehow became even closer when they learned they were brothers."

"Wait a minute. Learned they were brothers? What do you mean?"

"They're really half-brothers. Must be a story your dad left out."

"He didn't go into details, but he always told me granddad's faith was so strong because of how much grace God showed him when he found salvation."

"Oh, you don't know the half of it. He was far from being a saint when he came into our lives. My grandfather was very much the same. His faith was so very strong, but my father's faith was so very incredible. He was growing stronger spiritually every day."

"That makes sense. Dad told me he was almost singlehandedly behind turning the town around to follow the straight and narrow. Probably why the government came after our town first. From what I've been told, granddad was quite vocal in his rebellion against the government when it came to practicing his faith."

"So it's really illegal to be a Christian now?"

"That was the primary purpose behind the laws they made, to do away with Christianity, but they included any other kind of religion, too. They set the government up as the sole provider and god of the people."

"And the people just rolled over and let it happen?"

"Not everyone. I think you got to see up close what happened to anyone that disagreed."

"Oh yeah, right. Their 'machines.' They do this everywhere in the country, then?"

"Yes they do. Always make a big show of it in every community. It doesn't happen much anymore, though. Most Christians have been killed, and the rest of us hide out any way we can. We've had a few people betray us, but we've had more people join us."

Eli stepped forward and extended his hand out to Joshua for a handshake. "Forgive me for doubting you. It's just that I'm just suspicious about strangers."

"That's alright, Eli," said Joshua as he grasped Eli's hand in a firm handshake, "I understand."

"Eli has more reason to be suspicious than the rest of us. Two of his brothers were turned in for the reward money by traitors."

Sheila gave Eli a big hug. "You poor thing! That had to be so very hard for you!"

Jim turned to Joshua and winked. "Looks like your friend is starting to feel the compassion of the Spirit rising up in her."

"It's a definite change from the person I started this whole adventure with."

"I always like to see the change in a person after they let the Spirit inside. Watch over her and see the flame keeps growing. You know, our group could use people like you two, and I'd be honored if you joined us."

"I wish we could. But I have a feeling our journey needs to continue. This isn't our destination."

"I had a feeling you'd say that. What comes next for you two?"

"I think we need to get back to the tunnel. It's time to see what God has in store for us."

"I had a feeling you were going to say that, too."

Jim went to his desk and pulled out a map. "We need to plan this carefully."

Joshua was puzzled. "What do you mean?"

"The tunnel you speak of, the place where you were captured, is a very heavily guarded area. If we're to get you back there, we'll have to come up with a plan."

Sheila spoke up. "If it's dangerous, we can't ask you to do that. I mean, to risk anything for us. Maybe we should just stay here and join your gang."

Jim turned and faced her with a solemn look on his face. "No. I don't think so. As much as I'd like to welcome you two into the fold, I know deep down inside your job isn't done. And I also know we're going to do whatever we need to do to get you where God wants you to be."

"But you might be risking your lives."

"If necessary, so be it. But remember, it's a miracle you're here, so there may be another miracle waiting to get you out."

Eli spoke up. "That's right, we all know our life here is temporary. I'm with Jim on this one. God doesn't create a miracle like bringing you guys here without a greater purpose in mind for His glory. It's our duty to advance His kingdom, by doing what we can to help you keep His master plan in motion."

Joshua joined in. "Sheila, I don't want these guys to risk themselves for us any more than you do, but they're both right. It's our destiny to get back to the tunnel. Who knows, maybe the whole thing was just to bring you to Jesus and we'll be going home this time."

Jim interrupted and pointed his index finger skyward. "The bottom line is that someday we'll all be home. And together. That's all that matters."

"Amen!" shouted Eli.

"It's settled then," said Jim, "we do this thing."

"Yes," added Joshua, "we do it."

Sheila was puzzled. "I don't get you guys. I don't get it at all. But something inside me says it's the right thing to do."

"That's the Holy Spirit talking to you Sheila," said Joshua, "remember what it feels like so you can recognize that still, small voice that will guide you."

"I have so much to learn."

"We all do," said Jim, "we all do. Never stop learning His ways because there's more there than we can ever imagine in a million years. Now, it's getting late. How about you two get some sleep and let Eli and me work on getting this plan together so we can get you guys back to the tunnel. There's a room down the hall with a couple of cots in it. Not exactly deluxe accommodations, but you should be able to get some sleep."

Sheila let out a big yawn. "Sleep does sound good. Rest hasn't been something that's happened much during this journey. I don't know how we can ever repay you for everything you guys are doing for us."

Jim laughed. "There's only one thing you can do that will please me. You made a big decision back there during the trial tonight. You decided to follow Jesus and change your life forever. I just ask you to keep seeking Him and His guidance. That's the best thing you can do. From the stories my dad told me, this guy you're traveling with can show you the way."

Joshua blushed. "I'm nothing special."

"You're right. You're not. But letting the Holy Spirit do

special things through you is what makes the difference. Now both of you get out of here and get some sleep. Tomorrow will be a big day for you. Maybe for a lot of us."

12 THE GREAT ESCAPE

Joshua awoke from the sound of a quiet knocking on the door of the room they were sleeping in. He didn't know how long the quiet knocking had been going on. The cot wasn't especially comfortable, but knowing they were safe allowed him to settle into a deep sleep almost as soon as he lay down. A dim candle burning on the table gave him enough light to see that Sheila was still asleep in her cot at the other side of the room. He slipped off his blanket as quietly as possible, doing his best not to wake her up. As he slowly swung his leg off the cot and onto the floor, the stiffness and aches he felt were not-so-subtle reminders of the events of the day before. The pain in his legs made it hard to walk quietly, but each passing step made it easier as his aching muscles stretched out to normal. He turned the knob on the door as slowly as he could and hoped the creaking hinges weren't loud enough to wake Sheila as he stepped out into the hall. Jim was there to meet him with a big smile.

"I think we have a strategy worked out that will get you guys back to the tunnel safely. I would've liked to let you stick around longer, but we've got to act at a specific time to make this work. There's just enough time for you guys to have a bit of lunch before we get going."

Joshua rubbed his eyes. "Uh, Lunch? What time is it?"

"Nearly noon. You two went into hibernation pretty fast judging by how quickly we could hear you both snoring in there."

"Well, we needed the rest for sure." Both of them turned to see a still sleepy-looking Sheila standing at the door. "What's up?"

"Jim says he has a plan to get us back to the tunnel, but we have to eat and run to make it happen."

"Well, that shouldn't be a problem. Seems all we do is run, run, run."

"C'mon, you two. We have the table ready for you guys to eat. Time is of the essence."

Jim led them into another room in the mining tunnel that had a table and chairs set up. Joshua could see there were two plates there with food set on the table, ready and waiting for them.

"Wow, a spread fit for a king!" Joshua was excited when he saw the food set before them.

"Nothing but the best for my family! Dad told me that granddad liked bacon, so I thought you might too. We were able to get some eggs, fish, and apples to go with it."

Sheila had a look of surprise. "But I thought only government officials could get meat around here these days?"

"Let's just say a certain government official in a nearby town woke up to find out he had to be a vegetarian today." Jim laughed at his own joke.

"Rob from the rich and give to the poor, eh?"

"Oh, I wouldn't say 'rob,' I'd say we just borrowed a few things they could spare," said Jim with a wink.

"Something is oddly familiar here, but I can't put my finger on it," said Joshua.

"Probably the chairs. They were liberated from granddad's house after the trouble."

"Well, I'll be. They are the old chairs! My father found them set out on the curb for garbage and he brought them home and fixed them up. You see this? Right here on the back of the chair. This is where he carved 'J 3:16' into them for a reminder of God's greatest gift every time we sat down to eat."

"I always suspected something like that and now you've confirmed it. It just makes these chairs all the more special knowing granddad had a part in what they are. I'll feel like he's sitting here with me every time I eat now."

"I feel like he's here with us right now."

"I don't know if he is or not, but I can really feel the presence of the Spirit here today. We'll need every bit of the Spirit's guidance to pull this off without a hitch."

"Isn't there a way that's not dangerous?" asked Joshua between bites of egg and bacon.

"I'm afraid not. The tunnel's pretty heavily guarded all the time. I never could figure out why, but now I think it's a part of the enemy's plan to try and prevent whatever God is using it for. And you're part of God's plan in using it. I'm certain of it now. Eli thinks so too. He and others are already out there putting pieces of the plan together, getting things ready."

"Are you confident this plan will work?"

"I have some surprises in store for our 'friends' on the other side. It should give us an edge. We need to be going. Timing is a critical part of this plan. You'll see when we get there."

Sheila gulped down her last bit of egg. "I'm ready! Good night's sleep and a full stomach, so I'm ready for anything!"

Jim cackled, "that's the spirit! Let's get started!"

"Hold up a second, we better say a prayer for protection before we start." Joshua had a solemn look on his face.

Jim straightened up to full height. "You're right. We need to do this right." Jim reached into his pocket and pulled out a piece of paper.

"What's that?" asked Sheila.

"It's a copy of Psalm 91. Full of promises of God's protection for us. I like to read it when the going gets tough, and today will be a good excuse. Let's agree on these words of protection as I read them."

"Amen to that," said Joshua.

Joshua and Sheila both bowed their heads as Jim read the Psalm aloud. Sheila felt a calm and peacefulness like she'd never felt before settle over her as she listened to the words. It was if they were written for just how she was feeling that moment. Now she really was ready to face anything.

After the prayer, Jim lit a torch and led them down another passageway in the mine. There were so many twists, turns, and different passageways as they walked along, Joshua was certain he'd never be able to get out of the maze on his own. It was a good thing Jim knew the way. After what seemed like several miles of walking through the darkened passageways, Jim signaled to Joshua and Sheila to be quiet and still. He handed the torch to Joshua and seemed to almost quietly disappear right into the wall. A few moments later he appeared as quietly as he had left.

"We're clear. No one is out there."

"How did you do that?" asked Joshua.

"You mean this?" Jim stuck his hand into the wall. "We've gotten really good at camouflage after years of being in hiding."

"No kidding," Sheila said, "it looks like magic!"

"Follow me and I'll show you my next magic trick."

Jim led Joshua and Sheila through the wall, which turned out to be an intricate construction of plants that actually covered an entrance to the mine. They followed him quietly for a short distance where Jim stopped and stepped behind a few trees.

Jim whispered to them softly, "you guys ready for the next trick?"

Both Joshua and Sheila nodded, anxious to see what

Jim held in store. Neither of them expected him to reach over and pull a wall of vegetation aside to reveal a large drain culvert.

"Are we going to be hiding in there next?" asked Joshua.

"Oh no, I'm hiding something in it. This is an old drain system for the old superhighway. We use it for a variety of purposes when it suits our needs. But, wait till you see what's in here. Should be a big surprise for everyone."

Jim could tell by the looks on their faces they weren't expecting his surprise. Their faces were lit up with a combination of shock and excitement as Jim wheeled out the old motorcycle.

"Ladies and gentlemen, I present your escape vehicle!"

Joshua couldn't believe what he was hearing. "What? How is that old thing part of the plan?"

"It's going to be how we get you past the guards into the tunnel. It's going to be a tight squeeze, but the three of us can fit on it. Barely."

"You mean that thing still runs? And what about gas? I thought only government officials had gas!"

"Well, your dad, my grandad, built a really good bike and my dad taught me how to take care of it, so I've always kept it in running condition. As for gas, well, let's just say we 'liberated' some for our use."

"So the plan is you just drive us right up to the tunnel?"

"There's a little more to it than that. We have one team in the next town to the east set to raise a ruckus and draw some of the guards over there. Ten minutes later, we have another team in the next town to the west set to do the same thing and draw a few more guards away. That should only leave the guards stationed in the top of the tunnel in the old offices. Next, we have people posted at each side of the tunnel ready with explosives to draw the attention of the remaining guards off to the sides. As soon as all that takes place, we've calculated the sun will be shining directly towards them. I'm hoping with all that excitement, the shock of the sound of the motorcycle, and the sun at our backs, we can pull it off by roaring right down the middle of the road into the tunnel."

"Sounds a little iffy to me."

Jim laughed. "It is iffy. But if God shows up and shows off His power a little bit, it will be a piece of cake. Now if you'll give me a hand, we'll get this thing pushed into position. We're going to hide behind those bushes up ahead there and wait for the fun to begin."

"But how will we know when everything is going to happen?"

"It's a synchronized effort. We're all operating on the same time schedule. That way we won't have to be in contact. Of course, the down side of that is not knowing if some sort of glitch happens on the other end to slow things down or even prevent them from happening. There's a lot of faith involved."

Joshua laughed. "Sounds an awful lot like everyday life. A lot of faith involved."

"It doesn't take long being around you two to figure out you both fell out of the same family tree. It's so amazing how much you guys are alike even though you were born so many years apart," said Sheila.

The three of them worked at pushing the motorcycle into position as quietly as possible for their escape attempt. The bushes Jim had picked out to hide behind were in perfect position to be aligned with the opening of the tunnel and also provide a good vantage point to watch all the guards.

Jim looked at his watch. "Time for the first wave of the plan."

Almost as if on cue, the three of them watched from their hiding place as several of the guards at the front of the tunnel communicated between themselves and left immediately. Sheila was scared when the carriage carrying the guards went by their hiding place, but neither Jim nor Joshua seemed to show any anxiety as the guards passed by. She admired the courage these two guys displayed, a courage that seemed to come from the bond they shared with their Creator. She vowed to herself on the spot to learn to have the strength of faith that both Jim and Joshua displayed.

Jim looked at his watch again. "Time for wave two. Let's see if it works as well as the first wave did."

They watched the scene play out just as it did before. One of the guards appeared to receive a call and went over to the other. Both of them hopped into another carriage, and just as the others had done, traveled right past their hiding place. Now all that was left were the guards above the tunnel.

"Okay. Let's get ready. The third wave should be starting soon."

As Jim was starting to get Sheila positioned on the motorcycle, Joshua suddenly exclaimed, "Look! Look there!"

Jim and Sheila both looked to see what Joshua was pointing at. They both saw it at the same time. The fog was forming at the mouth of the tunnel.

"Do you see it?" asked Joshua, "it's the fog we see every time we enter the tunnel, only this time it's starting before we get there."

"Yes, yes it is Joshua!" exclaimed Sheila, "why do you think it's doing that?"

Jim chuckled. "So this is the fog you guys are talking about?"

"Yes, that's it. We've never seen it like this before though."

Jim chuckled again. "Well, I'll tell you what it is. I've seen it before. That, boys and girls, is the glory of the Lord descending upon us. I've seen it on several of the raids we've run before. It means He's here with us. God's joining in with the third wave! We're assured of a victory! Watch Him show off! Yeehaa!"

Jim just kept getting more excited as he got Joshua and

Sheila situated on the motorcycle. All the while they watched as the fog kept getting thicker and started swirling up around the guards. Just as the fog reached the guards and started to wrap around them, the party on the right side of the tunnel started to set off explosives. That was Jim's cue to bring the motorcycle to life. It was tight with all three of them on it, but Jim didn't seem to mind. He was crouched up upon the fuel tank, Sheila and Joshua both behind him hanging on as best they could.

"Hang on guys, here we go, right at 'em!"

The motorcycle roared to life as Jim hit the throttle and aimed it right towards the tunnel. Almost as soon as they started, the group on the left side of the tunnel started setting off their explosives. The guards were now not only distracted by explosions on both sides of the tunnel, they were also nearly blinded by the fog swirling around them and the sunlight in their eyes. There was no way they could even know what was going on as the roaring motorcycle with the driver screaming a war cry was speeding right at them.

To Sheila, it seemed like everything was moving in slow motion, but in reality, they were inside the tunnel in no time at all.

Jim slowed the motorcycle down to a smooth stop. "Well. This is it. We're in the tunnel and surrounded by the glory of the Lord! Yeeha! Did you see how He had our back? Yahoo!"

Sheila, a little bewildered, replied, "I wish I could be as enthused about this as you are, Jim. We're here. Again. With no idea what's coming up next. It scares me."

"Well, little lady, every time I've seen this glory surrounding us on a raid, good things happen. Miracles. Things mortal man can't pull off. Your presence here is proof that God has some sort of big plans for you two."

"You think so?"

"I know so. Why else would God grant me the blessing of meeting my great uncle years and years after he was supposed to be dead? Praise God for the miracle! Yeeha!"

"You're really acting so much like my father, it's uncanny."

"I guess the apple doesn't fall far from the apple that fell from the tree."

"I hate to be a third wheel, but now that we're here and we've made it, what next?" asked Sheila.

"Well," said Jim, "I guess it's time for me to turn this bike around and go back to my world and let you two go on to whatever the Lord above has planned for you next."

"You're not coming with us?" Sheila was beginning to enjoy the interaction between Jim and Joshua and really enjoyed hearing stories of their family.

"No, my place is back with my crew. We're still running the good race trying to bring the message of God's grace back to the country who's turned their back on Him. Before it's too late and there's no country left at all."

Joshua nodded his head. "I understand, Jim. I feel strongly that Sheila and I are meant to keep moving forward on our own journey. You can't do it for us, but I'm not going to lie and say I wouldn't have enjoyed having you along for the ride."

"I'll never forget you, uncle. Never. And if the good Lord ever sees fit to bless me with children, I'll be sure to tell them stories about you and our adventure together." Jim stuck out his hand for a handshake.

"Thanks, Jim. I don't know where we're heading, but wherever it is, I'll never forget you either." The two men shook hands, and knowing that wasn't enough, gave each other a good-bye hug.

"Miss Sheila, it's been a pleasure. I don't know what lies ahead for you, but the Lord will take care of you. And so will this guy you're traveling with."

"It's been a pleasure meeting you too, Jim. I can never thank you enough for what you've done for us."

"No thanks necessary, little lady. We're all working together for the Lord. All the glory belongs to Him."

With that, Jim gave a final wave and sent the motorcycle flying back towards where they came from, the front wheel rising off the ground in a dramatic wheelie. The echoing sounds of his bike and loud holler of victory echoed inside the tunnel long after they knew he was gone.

13 A NEW FRIEND

"Joshua, you never told me your family was so interesting."

"You didn't ask."

"I should smack you a good one. But, and I have a hard time saying this, after what we just went through, I feel like I'm closer to you now."

"Well. You are my sister now."

"Sister?"

"Oh, yeah. Sister in the Lord. Like it or not. You made a decision and now we're part of the same family."

"I think I like that idea. I think I could get used to it."

"Well, good, because it's a commitment that will last for all eternity. We may as well get going into our fog and see what comes at us next."

"What did Jim call it? It wasn't fog."

"You're right! He called it the Glory of the Lord surrounding us. You know, I think that makes me feel a whole lot better when I think of it that way."

"Me too. I'm still scared, but not as much. How about you lead the way?" Joshua could tell by the tone of her voice that Sheila was being sarcastic.

"The monsters always pick off the last person, you know."

"Enough of that talk, wise guy. We'll do this together."

"Yeah. You, me…and the Father, the Son, and the Holy Spirit!"

"Sounds like a regular party when you put it like that."

The two of them took the usual short steps in the fog since they couldn't see where they were going very well. Joshua even wondered if it mattered which direction they were going as long as they were in the fog. He figured it would take them where it wanted them to go.

"Do you see that, Joshua? The fog is thinning out, but these don't look like the tunnel walls. What do you think is going on?"

"I don't know. It looks about the same size and shape though. Maybe it will look different when we get outside. We're just about there."

As the two of the reached the outside of the tunnel, they noticed it certainly looked different on the outside too. The road stretched out before them, clean and pristine. The surface was definitely different than anything they'd ever seen before. Neither concrete or asphalt, it was a light-colored substance of some sort, almost resembling sand in its' appearance, yet with a type of translucent quality.

"Well, by the looks of things, we must be in the future this time, Sheila. Everything seems to be really different."

"This is crazy. Instead of falling apart, it looks like it's all been rebuilt. Everything looks so modern and futuristic."

"Yeah. I'd never believe the old tunnel would end up like this. But there's another thing that's weird about this whole thing here."

"What's that?"

"Everything is all fixed up for people to use. But just where is everyone? Be still and see if you can hear anything."

The two of them stood there silently for a moment, turning towards different directions to try and pick up even the slightest bit of a sound.

"I'm not hearing anything, Joshua. A little wind through the trees, but that's about it."

"It's pretty weird. Back in our own time, there were moments like this if there were no other hikers around, but there's been way too much effort put into this place for there to be no activity. At least, I'd think something should be going on somewhere."

"Yeah, I think so too. They wouldn't put so much money and effort into this place and not be using it. What do you think we should do?"

"We have two choices. We can turn back a little and maybe explore the facility or we can walk ahead and see what comes to meet us. So far, we haven't really had to go out looking, people have always come to us."

"Yeah, that's for sure. We certainly haven't had to wait very long before something happens each time we've come out of that stupid tunnel."

"Hey! Look over there! I think I see something familiar!"

Sheila looked over to where Joshua was pointing. It looked like a big rock at first and then the realization of what it was hit her.

"That's our monument, isn't it?"

"Or at least what's left of it. I'm not sure just how I feel about them not keeping our monument up after all these years."

"Well, I'm okay with it going away. I'm okay with going back home and forgetting all this."

"I think it's just like Jim said, we have a purpose in God's plan and the purpose isn't finished yet."

"Do you think we're far enough in the future that Jim isn't around anymore?"

"I've no way of knowing, but it looks like we're a pretty good piece into the future. I doubt he's still here."

"I wonder how things there worked out? Think we'll ever know?"

"That would probably depend on whether the good guys beat the bad guys or not. For all we know we might be heading towards being arrested again."

"I certainly hope not. I don't ever want to go through anything like that again."

"Me either. Even if Jim were here, I think he'd be too old to bail us out this time. I guess we should just start walking and see what happens."

"Joshua, I'm a little new to this, but shouldn't we say a prayer of some type before we start?"

"Yes, you're absolutely right. Would you like to lead us?"

"No. I don't know the right words. I've never said a real prayer before. You know how to do it."

"It's just talking to God. No special formula or words are required. Just tell Him what's on your mind. That's all He wants."

"It's really that simple?"

"Yep. Just tell him what's on your mind." "Well, if you say so."

"I say so."

"Okay. Here we go. Let's pray. Dear God, it's me, Sheila, with my friend Joshua. I don't know you nearly as well as Joshua does, but I know you're there now. I'm scared, but Joshua helps me to know I need to trust you. Help me do that. Help us know what to do and please protect us, okay? Thanks. Amen. How was that?"

"Perfect. You did an awesome job for your first time. It couldn't have been better."

"Thanks. I hope it gets easier as I go along."

"Oh, it will. Soon you'll be talking to God all the time."

Sheila laughed. "I hope I don't bore him to death."

"This is so strange. All this scenery is so very different, yet at the same time, it feels familiar."

"Yes. I wonder if this place became a tourist attraction. This road is nice, but it's not nearly big enough to use as a regular highway. Yet it looks too good for just a hiking trail."

"I agree. Say, isn't this about the spot where we ran across that woman along the road?"

"Yes, I think you're right. There are some of the same wildflowers around, but the landscaping is totally different."

Suddenly a shrill noise came from behind them, scaring them enough to make both of them jump. They turned around to discover a tear-shaped object that was about the size of a small car. The surface had a look that was both shiny and translucent appearing, yet they could not see through it.

"What is it Joshua?"

"I don't know. I guess we'll soon see. Whatever it is, I hope it's friendly. We better not move until we see something happening."

The two of them stood motionless, barely breathing before the strange object. Slowly the top started to open up, folding over to the side, and at the same time, the side of the object started to fold downward and tuck underneath the object.

"Hello there!" It was a feminine voice that greeted them from inside the object. Joshua and Sheila exchanged glances of surprise as neither of them was expecting a voice of greeting.

"Hello to you as well!" Joshua did his best to sound as friendly as possible since they still didn't know what they were facing.

A feminine head, followed by a thin body, emerged out of the object and stood before them. The person was wearing what looked like a jumpsuit of some kind, but the material was eerily similar to the object she arrived in.

"My name is Adriel. It's really a surprise to see someone else out here."

"My name is Joshua, and this is my friend Sheila."

"Joshua and Sheila, that's a strange, strange coincidence, those names. Well, I'm pleased to meet you both. May I be so bold as to ask what you two are doing out here?"

Joshua wasn't really sure how to best answer the question. The look on Adriel's face when she learned their names concerned him. "Please don't take this the wrong way. But we really can't explain why we're here. Don't worry, we're completely harmless. Really, we are."

"Okay. So let's say I let that slide. Can you at least tell me why you're wearing such strange clothing? If I didn't know better, I'd say you raided a museum to get those."

"The best explanation I can give for the clothes is because we're, um, not really from around here."

"Yeah," chimed in Sheila, "we're from a different place altogether."

Adriel looked at the two of them carefully. She then reached into her pocket and pulled out a small rectangular thing and pointed it at them. They couldn't tell what the thing was, but she seemed to be satisfied when it began to softly glow blue.

"You check out as being honest. I won't pry too much about why you can't explain your presence. I also have my own sense about reading people and I think you two are probably okay people. I can give you a lift to where you're going if you like."

"We really don't have anywhere we're going." Sheila realized as soon as the words left her mouth she probably shouldn't have said anything.

"Wait a minute. First you can't tell me why you're here. Then you can't tell me where you came from. Now you're telling me you aren't going anywhere?"

"Well, like I said before, I really can't explain why we're here."

"Answer me this. Do you have a place to stay?"

"No, no we don't."

"Then I insist you come with me. Those of us that are left must stick together."

Joshua was puzzled. "What do you mean by 'those of

us that are left?' That sounds pretty ominous."

"Geez. How could you not know? Have you been living under a rock or something?"

"Or something pretty much sums it up."

"I can see I'm going to have to drag every little bit of information out of you. Hop on into my transporter and we can talk on the way."

Sheila turned and looked at Joshua. "Do you think we should?"

"I don't have a better idea, so why not?"

"Good, it's settled then," said Adriel, "hop in and we'll get going."

The inside of the transporter was like nothing Joshua had ever seen before. The front two seats were side by side and the third seat was in the middle between the two front seats. The layout of the interior was similar to the cars he was familiar with, but looked nothing at all like a car inside. Instead of the gauges and switches he was used to on the dash, the front of the transporter had a curved panel of lights and buttons with no trace of a steering wheel. From the inside of the transporter, the whole top half looked like a tinted window, except there were no bars or pillars, it was just like sitting inside a bubble.

"You seem to be mesmerized, Joshua. Surely you've been in a transport before. It's not like this is one of the newer, fancy ones either."

"I... uh... can't say that I've ever been in one of these before."

"I see how it is. Let me get this thing going and we'll talk." Adriel turned towards the front of the transport and spoke. "Transport A7A3. Junction 7. Stop17."

Joshua didn't understand the commands, but as soon as Adriel spoke, the transport started to move. He could understand now how they couldn't hear it coming up behind them before because it seemed to be noiseless as it started moving down the road. Neither he nor Sheila could get over the view from the top of the transport. It was truly like traveling in a giant bubble. As soon as the transport started to move, Adriel turned her seat so she could face both Joshua and Sheila at the same time.

"Okay, let's start talking. I want to figure out what's going on with you guys. Maybe I can help."

Sheila interrupted, "before you launch into whatever it is you have to say, can you please tell me who's driving this thing?"

Adriel shook her head. "You two really are an oddity. The transporter has sensors to read the travel lanes and all I have to do is tell it the destination and it takes off. I don't see how you guys have gotten to the age you are without knowing this stuff."

"Wow, that's crazy," said Sheila.

Adriel continued, "I have an idea that might help us here. I'll tell you what I'm going to do. I'm going to tell you all about me, and then maybe you can trust me enough to tell me more about yourselves. Okay?"

"Sounds like a plan," said Joshua, "we'll see where it leads."

"Okay, here goes. I'm a researcher. I work and live in the next town. I've lived around here my whole life. I've never been married, but I hope something happens to change that someday. The destination I gave the transport is where I work. I pretty much live there now."

"You live where you work?" asked Joshua.

"Right now it just seems more efficient. I've been working around the clock, so I just sleep there too. It's not like there's anyone else around, anyway. There's enough room for you two there if you need to spend the night. I'm only out here now because I needed to borrow some tools from the hospital that I needed."

"Couldn't they have just shipped what you needed over?"

"If I didn't know any better, I'd say you didn't know."

"I'm pretty sure I don't know, whatever it is. Please explain it to us."

"You know. The plague. There's not a lot of us left, you know. That's why I was so surprised to see the two of you. I haven't seen anyone else around here for a long time. It's also why we can use this travel lane. It was off limits to transports and designated for tourist use only. I figured it was okay since there's no one else around to use it."

Joshua and Sheila looked at each other and then looked at Adriel. "The plague?"

"We're here now. Let's go up to my office and we'll discuss things further."

Adriel turned her seat around to face the front once more. "Transport. Egress."

The doors of the transport opened just as they had seen when Adriel came across them. Joshua could see the building it parked at looked to be made of a material similar to what the road they traveled on was made of, although the coloring was different. Adriel led them to the front door which turned out to be only a few feet from the transport.

"Stick to me closely when I open this door. The security system won't let you in if you're too far behind."

Joshua and Sheila watched as Adriel looked directly into a black rectangle on the wall of the building while at the same time holding her right palm against another black rectangle down below the first one. From seemingly out of nowhere, a door opened in the side of the wall.

"Come on, follow me."

Adriel led them over to a wall that was lined with openings that Joshua guessed were elevators of some sort.

"This one is ours right here. Come on in, it's quite alright." Adriel turned to a small circular shape on the wall and spoke into it. "Floor D."

Joshua was expecting the feel of elevators he'd been in before. Instead, he couldn't even tell when this one started or stopped. If he hadn't seen the view outside the door change, he'd think they hadn't even moved yet.

"Welcome to my humble floor. Make yourselves at home."

Joshua and Sheila walked into the room and looked around. They could see an area in the corner where it looked like Adriel slept and prepared meals. The rest of the room appeared to be full of futuristic laboratory equipment. They were both nearly hypnotized by the complexity of what they were looking at.

"This... this is all so incredible." Sheila was still overwhelmed by the sight of everything.

"Since you two obviously don't belong here and don't have anywhere to go, why don't you stay here with me? I can put up some more places to sleep and there's more than enough food."

"I don't think we could repay that kind of hospitality," said Sheila, "you're being very kind."

Joshua had a sudden thought and spoke up. "Actually, I think we can repay you."

Sheila wasn't sure what he meant until she saw him reach into a small compartment in his backpack and pull out one of the gold coins they had gotten earlier.

"Here," he said as handed the coin to Adriel, "we can give you this."

Adriel took the coin and looked at it. Then she looked at Joshua and Sheila. Then she looked at the coin. All the color seemed to be draining from her face.

"You..."

Adriel couldn't finish her sentence. She clutched the coin tightly and held it to her chest, appearing to be trying to catch her breath. She kept looking back and forth between the two of them looking like she'd seen a ghost or monster.

"You... you two have to come with me to my office."

Joshua and Sheila followed Adriel to a small room at the rear of the one they were in. She was still looking at the two of them in disbelief.

"Where did you get this coin? Can you tell me?"

Joshua looked down at the floor. "I could tell you, but I don't think you'd believe it."

Adriel leaned in closer to Joshua and spoke softly. "I want to know if it came from the same place...as that one."

Joshua and Sheila looked to where Adriel was pointing. There on the wall behind her was the same kind of coin, framed in a special frame. It especially stood out because the frame was the only thing they'd seen there that didn't look futuristic.

Joshua's curiosity was aroused. "Where'd the one you have come from?"

"It's been passed down from generation to generation. My great-great-great grandmother saved it to remember the one who gave it to her along with some others to help her out. I heard the story many times when I was a little girl. She got the coin from... a young man named Joshua. A young man named Joshua who was traveling with a young girl named Sheila. And I have to know. You have to tell me. By some miracle of God, are you that Joshua?"

Joshua was shocked to hear the story, but it had to be true. It was just much of a coincidence not to be. "Was your great-great-great grandmother's name... Emily? Emily Swanson?"

Adriel gasped loudly. "Yes, yes it was! I have a picture of her in my desk drawer."

Adriel sat down at her desk and opened up a drawer on the side and brought out a small, wooden box and placed it on top of the desk. Flipping the lid open, she pulled out what as a very obviously old photograph that appeared to be encased in some kind of plastic.

"Here. Here is what she looked like."

Joshua moved in for a closer look. "Yes, that's Emily alright. You were talking about her back along the road, Sheila, and now here she is in this picture!"

"Yes, that's her alright. I remember."

Adriel was visibly moved. A tear rolled down her cheek and she gave an astonished Joshua a very big hug.

"It's real. You're really the one! It was starting to creep me out with your names and the old clothes, but when you pulled out that coin, I knew it really had to be you!"

Joshua was clearly uncomfortable. "Yes, it's me, but what's the big deal?"

"Because of you, I'm here today and I am what I am. Because of you!"

"Wow. You're going to have to slow down a little and explain yourself a bit."

"I'll tell you the story we've handed down for generations. Grandma Emily had herself convinced to have an abortion or maybe even do something worse. She had pulled off the road in desperation when this stranger named Joshua came along from out of nowhere with a smart-alecky girl named Sheila." Adriel paused from the awkward statement. "Oh, I'm sorry Sheila, I hope that didn't offend you."

"No offense taken. I've changed a little since then." Joshua nodded enthusiastically in agreement.

"Anyway, the story always told how you, Joshua, talked some sense into her and made her think. Then you gave her money and an idea of where to go find a pastor that would help her. She was scared and changed her mind when she got to the church, so she went right on by the church and decided to keep on going. She didn't get very far till she had a flat tire and pulled over. A kindly man stopped to help and changed the tire for her. She felt at ease around him while he was changing the tire and started telling him about her troubles. Wouldn't you know it turned out the kindly gentlemen turned out to be the pastor of the church she had just passed by. He and his wife took in Grandma Emily and in another stroke of divine providence, a member of the congregation was a coin collector and volunteered to help her sell the coins and get the most possible money out of them. She made a vow right then and there to keep one of the coins as a reminder of how God led her through her troubles by placing other people in her path to help. From that moment onward, she took full responsibility for her actions and gave birth to my great-great grandmother, Helen. The whole congregation adopted both of them as their own and helped provide for them till they were established enough to take care of themselves. From the time Grandma Helen was a small child, Grandma Emily taught her this story so she'd always know God was there to help and might even use her to help others. The story inspired Grandma Helen so much, she grew up and became a doctor, as did my great grandfather, my grandfather, and my mother. The inspiration of my ancestors is why I became a medical researcher. It all started because you stopped along the road to help someone. If not for you, there probably wouldn't have been a Grandma Helen, and that would trickle on down to me not existing today."

"Wow. I guess we never know how many lives we ultimately touch through the ages. I can't help but notice you speak of God and miracles, too. Are you a Christian? Is it okay to be a Christian here?"

Adriel laughed. "Of course I'm a Christian. And of course it's okay. Most people these days recognize the intelligent design behind everything that exists. And you're right about not knowing how many people we touch through the ages. I'm not bragging, but consider how many people my family of doctors has helped through the years. All on account of your caring. But now, that may all come to an end. This plague I've been trying to find an answer to has taken a lot of people. That's why you haven't seen anyone else but me. The population has really thinned down from this thing."

Joshua was very solemn as he spoke, "I can't take the credit for the caring. That's just doing what Jesus would want me to do. Tell us more about this disease you're fighting."

"It started several years ago. We thought it was just a

few isolated cases, but after a few months it started to spread. Soon after that it became an epidemic and started spreading around the world. We have no clue how it's carried, why people catch it, or how to stop it." "It comes on suddenly with no warning, for no apparent reason. We can't find any connection to anything causing it. So far, the only thing that's predictable is the fact that it's always been fatal. Every time."

"Is it like a fever, a cancer?"

"No. The victims just gradually waste away till they pass. Just keep getting weaker and weaker till it's over."

Sheila's ears perked up. "And the skin? How does their skin look? What do they look like?"

"Well, it would turn a bluish tint, almost a like a green."

"Kind of like the skin of a fish?" asked Joshua.

"I guess you could say that," replied Adriel.

Sheila turned her face away so they wouldn't see the tears rolling down her cheeks. "That's what my sister has."

Joshua took off his backpack and opened up a tiny, hidden pocket within one of the compartments inside. "I don't know for sure, but I think I have something here that may help."

Adriel looked on with curiosity as Joshua pulled what appeared to be a small, leather bag from his backpack. Sheila's eyes lit up with the memory of where it came from.

"What is it you have there?" asked Adriel, the curiosity in her mounting.

"In this little bag, right here, may be the cure to your plague. A friend we met on our travels gave it to us and told us it cured what he called fish-skin sickness. Not only that, he told us it would cure lots of people."

"Let me see what we have here." Adriel peeked inside the bag. "What is this stuff?"

"Dried flower petals. Some sort of a blue flower, but I've never seen one like it anywhere else. I'm not sure if they even exist anymore. He told us the petals had to be made into a tea."

Adriel looked at the contents of the small bag carefully. It was obvious she was in deep thought, considering what Joshua had told her about the flower petals and what possibilities could exist for their use.

"If what your friend told you is true, this could be a major breakthrough. I think we can make this happen."

"But how can we make enough tea to help so many sick people with this small amount of petals?"

"With the technology and equipment I have here, I may be able to synthesize a formula that has the same properties. I've been looking at different natural elements for some time trying to unlock a cure, so I already have many of the tools in place to do the job."

"Do you think the chances of succeeding are very good?"

"Any chance is better than we've been doing so far. This is the first spark of hope I've had for a while."

"Can I do anything to help you?" asked Sheila.

"You just might be able to help out a little. The extra set of hands might come in handy."

"How about me? What can I do?" asked Joshua.

"I think Sheila's help will be all I need. You can take a nap over there on my cot if you like. The both of you look like you're in need of some rest."

"It has been quite a journey," admitted Joshua, "this is the most comfortable I've been for a while. A nap might just be what I need. And you are the doctor, so you know best." Joshua chuckled at his own remark.

"Well," Sheila replied, "I have to admit, they did take pretty good care of me while you were in jail. I'm sure I got a lot more rest then than you did."

"Jail?" exclaimed Adriel, "how did jail come into this story? You two must tell me of your adventures and how you ended up here. It has to be quite a miraculous tale."

"I'll tell you about it while we're working and Joshua catches some sleep. He's been carrying my load for a lot of our journey, so now it's my turn to pick up some slack. That's right, bub. You go over there and take a nap and we'll take it from here."

"I see how it is now. I'll just go over here quietly and go to sleep so I don't disturb you two or get in the way."

Joshua laughed the whole way to the cot. Fully relaxing for the first time in what seemed an eternity, he fell asleep in seconds. More than six hours of sound sleep had passed by when Sheila shook him awake.

"We did it! We did it! We did it!"

"Huh? What? Did what? Mom?"

Sheila laughed. "I'm not your mom, silly. Wake up! We did it! Adriel and I have a serum mixed up to try out on the disease."

Joshua had slept so deeply he was still having a little trouble getting acclimated to what was going on. "Huh? Disease? What's going on?"

Adriel handed Joshua some coffee. "Here this will help you wake up. Sheila and I got the formula synthesized. Now we get to try it out!"

The coffee helped Joshua wake up and remember what was going on. "You guys did it? Awesome! What come next?"

"I have some subjects I can try it out on down at the hospital. You guys can just crash here while I hop on over to JD3 Memorial and try this stuff out."

Joshua couldn't believe what he heard. "Wait a minute. JD3 Memorial? Does that name stand for what I think it does?"

"Well, it is kind of a nickname. The full name is James Dunning the Third Memorial Hospital."

Sheila shrieked. "Jim made it!"

Adriel had a confused look on her face. "You act as if you knew him."

Joshua answered. "We did. We did know him. He's the one who got us here. We weren't sure he made it back safely or not."

"Sheila told me about some of your adventures. I still have trouble wrapping my head around this whole thing. It's just crazy to think that a guy that's been gone so many years is responsible for you two standing before me today."

"Yeah. I know," replied Joshua, "it's strange, but true. We probably owe our lives to Jim."

"Well, let's hope this concoction works. That would be more than enough to pay off your debt to him if it did. Also a great way to honor his name, not that it needs any more honor."

"What do you mean?"

"Jim Dunning is the one who led the resistance in this area that defeated the government and brought back freedom of religion. Because of him, people of faith were able to worship again. Something the government almost succeeded in taking away and probably would have succeeded in if not for Mr. Dunning."

"That's incredible. From the little we knew him, he was definitely an incredible man, just like his grandfather. I have faith this cure will work, just like another incredible man, the one who gave it to us said it would."

"Well I'll share that faith, then, if that's the case. You two can just hang out here while I go over to the hospital and try this out."

"Sounds like a plan. I have a beauty nap to get back to." Sheila just rolled her eyes at Joshua's joke and laughed to herself.

14 ANOTHER MIRACLE

Joshua had no idea how long he had been asleep when the sound of the Adriel returning woke him up. He glanced over to where Sheila was and saw she was still sound asleep. He could see Adriel tip-toeing around to be as quiet as possible. Slowly he arose, as quietly as possible so Sheila wouldn't wake, and went over to where Adriel was.

"Oh I'm sorry, did I wake you?"

"Yes, but I think it was time for me to get up. This is the most refreshed I've felt since this whole thing started."

"Sheila told me of your adventures while we worked. I think you must possess the same kind of faith as James Dunning did."

"Did Sheila tell you why there might be a little bit of similarity there?"

"Well, no, she didn't mention any kind of connection."

"Jim Dunning, the first Jim Dunning, is my father."

"What? That's incredible! To think the two of you have been wandering around back and forth in time the way you have been, how so much of this is working together, it's just miraculous!"

"Miraculous is the right word. Only God could make something like this happen."

"Yes, I can't argue that. Especially after seeing how well your flower petal cure worked."

"Are you saying what I think you are? Your formula worked?"

"No, *your* formula worked. The flower petals from your friend. All I did was figure out how to synthesize it so we can produce it as we need it. And we'll be needing a lot."

"Are the people in the hospital going to make it?"

"Thanks to you, I'm pretty sure they will. After giving them some of your tea, they started to improve within an hour. We've never seen any kind of improvement in any of the previous patients before."

"That's awesome! Glory to God!"

"Yes, He certainly had to set this whole thing up. No way a human could have pulled this off."

"Hey, what's this I'm hearing? The tea solution we made last night worked?" Joshua and Adriel were so excited about what had taken place that they didn't even notice Sheila had woken up and came over to join them.

"Yes, Walking Bear's petals did the trick!"

"Uh, Walking Bear?" Adriel was intrigued by this new bit of information.

"I didn't think you'd believe it was legitimate if I told you we got them from an Indian medicine man," laughed Joshua.

"You do have a point there. I think that's a little detail I'll have to think about keeping to myself. I mean, really, who would believe the worst plague mankind has ever seen was ended by a Native American medicine man?"

"Who was shown the whole thing in a dream from God."

"Are you kidding me?"

"No, Adriel, he isn't kidding you, I was there, too. That's exactly what Walking Bear told us."

"Wow. I hope I'm not pressed too hard for details on this one. Who'd believe the cure came from an old medicine man and delivered by two time travelers? I'm a part of this and I have trouble believing it."

Joshua laughed. "You should try seeing it from our side."

"Yes, I imagine so. Can I talk you two into staying on here? I'm sure I could find you a place to stay."

"I appreciate the offer, Adriel, but I think my purpose here is done. It would be easier to stay here instead of facing the unknown, but I think I'm supposed to see what happens next. How about you, Sheila? I won't force you to come along. The choice is yours."

"Adriel, I can't even begin to tell you how much I enjoyed working with you here, but this isn't where I belong. My sister was dying from this disease when we left. I am still hoping somehow, some way, we can make it back. Now that we have a cure, we can save her if we ever get back there."

"I pretty well knew you guys wouldn't be staying, but I had to ask. I would've loved to have you here with me. I've taken the liberty of mixing some of the tea up for you guys to take with you. I figured it may come in handy wherever you end up."

"Sounds like you were prepared for our departure."

"Yes, but one more thing." Adriel reached into a pocket of her outfit. "Take this. It's directions for duplicating the tea synthetically. You may need that as well. It can be done without modern equipment, so you should stand a pretty good chance for making it wherever or whenever you land. Provided you don't end up back with the Native Americans again." Adriel gave them a playful wink when she mentioned being with the Indians.

The trio stood silently in the elevator, Joshua and Sheila ready to move on to the next step of their adventure, yet they were a little sad they had to leave their new friend so soon. Adriel was also wishing her new friends could stay longer. Even though they'd only been together a day, there was just something about how they interacted together making if feel like they'd all known each other for years.

"Ground," Ariel spoke into the elevator. It seemed like they were instantly on the ground level of the building with no hesitation.

"The transport is ready outside to take you guys back to that tunnel of yours."

"I have mixed feelings about that," replied Joshua. "Part of me wants to see what's next, but there's a part of me that wants to stay."

"Me too," said Sheila, "but I know going back is the right thing to do now."

Both of them looked back at the building as the doors to the transport opened up for them to get in. Knowing the lives their adventure had saved made this a special place and they wanted to fix it firmly in their memories.

"Well," said Adriel, "let's get this show on the road. All aboard the tunnel express!"

"I like the sound of that," said Joshua, "tunnel express has a certain kind of ring to it."

After they got into their seats, Adriel spoke the directions into the transport computer to set the course. Even though they had ridden in the transport before, both Joshua and Sheila were still amazed at how quietly it traveled and how good the view was. The transport had to be traveling twice as fast as the cars they were used to, but it was so smooth it felt like they weren't even moving. It was moving so fast, it was only a matter of moments till they arrived at the tunnel.

"Well, we're here," announced Adriel, "there's your tunnel."

"It looks so nice now compared to the entrance we left behind."

"A lot of effort went into preserving the history of it through the years."

"We've seen a lot of that history in a short time. You might be the only one we can share it all with," said Sheila.

"Yes, you've been a special friend to us Adriel," added Joshua, "you're right up there with the others who have helped along the way. But there just seemed to be a special connection between us."

The three of them exited the transport and stood to face the tunnel.

"I think I know why it was different this time," said Sheila. "This time I was working with you, Joshua, not against you."

"I hadn't thought of it that way. You weren't a believer till our last stop, so that might figure into it."

"Wait a minute," exclaimed Adriel, "you weren't a believer and he was when this thing started?"

"That's right," answered Sheila, "I learned what was real by following this guy around. And I was a real pain in the you know what till I figured it out."

"No comment," laughed Joshua.

Adriel sighed. "I almost wish I could come along with you. From what Sheila told me, there's been a lot of excitement."

Joshua got a stern look on his face. "Trust me, it hasn't been a lot of fun. God has always shown up to get us through it, but it's not been the easiest of things going through our trials and waiting for His timing."

"But yet watching how you handled yourself while we were waiting is what helped convince me that God is real," said Sheila, "you never once let our circumstances get to you. If it was all a fake show, you would've caved in to save yourself a lot of grief."

"Well," replied Joshua, "the original disciples went through far worse. If Jesus' sacrifice on the cross had been a made up story, they would've lied to save themselves. And they didn't. All of them stayed true to the end. People just don't die for a lie."

"That's right," said Adriel, "the disciples were there to see genuine miracles. And you know what? I got the opportunity to see a genuine miracle myself. A miracle you guys are living out. This is so very incredible. I don't know how I'll get anyone to believe an incredible story like this one."

Joshua opened up his backpack. "Here. Take this. You can show it off when you tell the story."

"The little leather bag you brought the petals in? Are you sure? I mean, your Indian friend gave it to you."

"Now that I think of it, he didn't really give it to me. It was to cure a terrible disease and I'm just the delivery boy. It really belongs to you."

"Wow, thanks! I'll be able to show off this Native American handiwork when I tell the story to my children if I ever have any. That should lend some authenticity to the tale. It's all so incredible, they'll think I'm nuts anyway. No one will believe all this."

"I have a feeling there will be children in your future, Adriel," said Sheila.

Joshua pointed towards the tunnel. "There's some more authenticity for you."

"Is that what I think it is?"

"Yes, that's the fog I told you about," replied Sheila.

"That is unbelievable! And this happens every time you enter the tunnel?

Adriel looked in amazement as the fog started to curl around the entrance of the tunnel.

"Is that the way it always looks?"

"Pretty close. When Jim drove us into the tunnel, it came out further to meet us. I think there's more of a glow to it now, too. Almost like its' got power within it."

"If you ask me, it does have a power within it. And a power behind it, too," replied Sheila.

"It's just so beautiful, so alive," exclaimed Adriel.

Joshua laughed. "I've never seen it that way before, because it always signified a trial ahead, but this time, I can definitely see it in a different way."

"Jim called it the Glory of the Lord," said Sheila quietly. "I can really feel that this time. It is truly a glory to behold."

"Adriel, thank you so much for bringing us here and thank you for everything you've done for us," said Joshua.

"Yes," added Sheila, "you've done so much for us. We can never repay you for your kindness."

Adriel laughed. "You two brought me a cure to end a massive plague, and you're thanking me? Now that's funny."

Joshua thumped his chest and pointed skyward. "It was all God, all the time. Every time."

"Now we get to see where God and this tunnel takes us to next, don't we?" Sheila had a concerned look on her face.

"Yes we do, Sheila. I'm sure God will keep on guiding us along the way. You look troubled, is there something wrong?"

"Well, yeah. I keep thinking of how I left Sarah, how sick she was, and how badly I had been treating my mom. I wish I could make it up to them somehow."

"I think we're seeing with God, anything is possible. So don't give up on anything. Pray about it. Once you're tuned in, He'll light your path and guide you."

"Start singing to me, and I'll slap you up alongside your head," laughed Sheila.

Joshua started to laugh too. "Yeah, I guess I was getting too close to song lyrics."

Adriel joined in the laughter. "You two crack me up. You make such a great team."

Joshua and Sheila looked at each other and blushed. Neither of them had thought of themselves as being a team before, although it was clear to Adriel that both of them liked the idea.

"We'd better get going and see what lies ahead," said Joshua, happy for the opportunity to change the subject.

"Yes, you're probably right," added Sheila, happy to change the subject as well.

"Come here you guys," said Adriel as she pulled them

in closely for a group hug. "Take care of yourselves."

"You too, Adriel," Joshua said as he waved goodbye. Sheila nodded and waved as she blinked back tears.

Adriel then watched as the pair walked into the fog. Their images slowly started to fade and then disappear as the fog totally enveloped them. As soon as they disappeared, the fog started to gradually fade away until it was all gone and the tunnel entrance looked normal. "Godspeed, my friends," Adriel whispered as tears started to roll down her cheeks.

Joshua and Sheila made their way through the fog, just as they did before. This time, it felt more familiar and comforting than it did in the past.

"Have any feelings about what will happen this time Joshua?"

"No. No I don't. But in a way, this almost feels comfortable now. With all the good that happened back there with Adriel, it really showed how God can really pull together things from out of nowhere and make things work, how he can use us to do his work."

"Yeah, it does. Has it always been this way for you? Could you always see God's hand in things?"

"No, not always. There were times I could really feel God's presence and know just what he wanted to do, and other times when I really didn't know what was going on till it was over. Kind of like what we just went through."

"It always seemed to me that you knew what you were doing. Like you knew what the plan was."

"No, I was just keeping the faith and putting one foot in front of the other, one step at a time. Sometimes that's all we can do."

"Well, it seems it was good enough so far. Hey, look there, it's a familiar face!" Sheila was pointing to the cartoon character on the wall of the tunnel they noticed when they first came into the tunnel.

"Yes it is. It's like… hey, you know what that means? It means we have to be pretty close in time to when we left.

That mural looks the same as it did when we left."

"Are you saying what I think you're saying? That we're home this time?"

"I don't want to get your hopes up just yet, but this is the first time we're not obviously in a different place. But if we're not home, we may not be very far from it."

"Dear God, please, please, please, please let this be home. Please!" Sheila's prayer was short, but Joshua could tell it was very sincere. It was also one he could definitely agree with.

"Amen to that," said Joshua.

"Look Joshua! The opening! Everything! It's all like we just left it!"

Sheila started dancing around out of happiness. Joshua felt like dancing, too, but he was still cautious, still studying everything around them, hoping not to find something different or out of place from when they first entered the tunnel.

"Stop being a Negative Nancy, Joshua, we're back! We're really back! Dance with me!"

"I know! I'll check my cell phone in my backpack!"

Joshua hurriedly dug into his backpack looking for his cell phone. Sheila looked at the expression on his face anxiously waiting to see if he had good news or bad news. Her chin started to quiver when she saw the frown on his face.

"Oh no… we're not home, are we?" Sheila's voice was shaking as she spoke.

"Battery's dead."

"What? Your battery is dead? I thought our hopes of being home were dashed and you're telling me your battery is dead? Why you…"

Sheila's voice trailed off. Her look of anger turned to one of embarrassment.

"I'm sorry, Joshua. I had a brief moment of the old me. I was going to launch into a bunch of nasty words then I remembered that's not who I am now."

"That's okay. We've been through a lot. You shouldn't expect to be in control every second."

"You seem to be."

"That's only what you see on the outside. Anyway, how about your cell phone?"

Sheila pulled out her phone and looked at it.

"Battery's dead."

Joshua started laughing. "I can't find anything to prove we're home for sure or anything to prove we're not. How about we just start walking and see if the car's waiting for us?"

"Well, that would probably be a good idea. It would be a good sign if no one met us too. Seems like every time we come out of the tunnel, trouble comes to meet us."

"Yeah, that's right. We never did have to wait long for trouble to find us. Let's get going."

The two set out walking, at a much faster pace than they had when they first hiked to the tunnel. Both of them scanned every tree, bush, or hole in the pavement looking for any signs of a change or difference since they left. It was so very hard to hold back the emotions that came with the hope of finally being back where they belonged, hoping the adventure was over and life would go back to normal.

Sheila turned and looked back. They had walked far enough that the tunnel was out of site around the bend in the road. "I really think we're back this time, Joshua."

"I don't want to jinx things by saying it, but I think we are too."

"I have to see if the car is still there!" Sheila took off running in the direction of where the car was parked.

"Sheila, wait! That's a long distance to run the whole way! Pace yourself!" Joshua watched helplessly as Sheila kept getting further and further away. With a shrug of his shoulders, he gave up and started running after her. "Hey! Wait up!"

Joshua was surprised how well Sheila ran. He was

having a little difficulty himself, still suffering from some of the bruises he had from being captured and had to slow to a walk occasionally. He caught up to Sheila in a few minutes, finding her sitting on the ground beside his car crying. He sat down beside her, almost breathless. She turned to look at him, still crying, and laid her head on his shoulder. After a minute or so, he regained his breath enough to speak.

"Are you okay?"

Sheila nodded back at him, still crying.

"What's wrong?"

"Here. The car is here. Just like we left it." Sheila had trouble talking through the tears.

"Yes, yes it is! Isn't that awesome?"

Sheila nodded again, trying to regain her composure. "That's when I realized it."

"I don't understand."

"This…this whole thing. It was for me. God did it all to get my attention. All of it. Just for me. I just…I just always thought that church stuff was for goody-good people. I never…I never knew God could care for me so much that He'd do all of this. Just for me."

"Yes, it's really a shocker when you realize it. Jesus died on the cross for you. And for me. It's really amazing that He died for all of mankind, but it's really a humbling experience when you realize that he didn't just die for mankind, he died for each person individually."

"I…I think I understand that now. But this is just so hard for me to wrap my head around all this. It's just so more than I could ever imagine."

"Yes it is. People just don't realize how much Jesus cares for them. He'd go to the gates of Hell to save a single person. The world tries to keep that truth away from everyone and say the government is all they need."

"Yeah, I guess we saw that with Jim, didn't we?"

"I didn't think of it that way before, but yeah, you're right. Anyway, don't you think we should get this cure back to your sister?"

"But what if…what if we're too late? We still don't know what time it is. Maybe it's the next day, or next week. What if she's already gone?" Sheila started crying again.

"But what if it's last week and she's not as sick? The evil one will try to get you to dwell on the negative. Let's just have faith we're right back where we started from."

Sheila nodded through the tears.

"You know what? There's a charger in the car, we can plug in one of our phones and see what time it is."

"We can do that on the way. Everything's going to be alright."

"That's the spirit!"

Joshua held the door open for Sheila as she got into the car and then went around to the other side and got in himself. After everything they'd been through it seemed so surreal to be back where they started from.

"Joshua?"

"Yes?"

"Do you mind if I say a quick prayer before we head back?"

"I think that's an excellent idea!"

"Dear Jesus, I can't understand why you did so much for me, so for now, I'm just going to thank you. Please let us get back safely and get to Sarah in time. Thanks. Amen."

"Amen. That was an awesome prayer, Sheila, right to the point."

"Thanks. Now let's get going!"

Joshua started up his car and pulled out of the parking lot. He had a greater appreciation for the scenery around them after their adventure, his head spinning with the images from his memory of all the people and things they'd seen each time they'd left the tunnel.

"Joshua? I just plugged in my phone and looked at the time. I don't remember for sure, but it looks like we're right back where we started from, the exact same time!"

"Praise God! Looks like there won't be any monuments to us anytime soon! Yahoo!"

"I'll be seeing that in my nightmares for a long time. What a horrible thing to see!"

"Yeah, you and me both. It still feels like being back here isn't real yet."

"Nothing's seemed real since…since…well, I don't know, we've been gone so long, but the clock says we haven't been, so I don't really know how long." Sheila laughed out loud at the thought of it.

"It is pretty hard to comprehend, isn't it?"

"For sure. Hey, are you exceeding the speed limit?"

"Well, yeah, I guess I am. Excited to get back to your sister and get that taken care of, I suppose."

"Well, just slow down and be safe. I don't want to have gone through all this only to end up wrapped around a tree!"

"Yes ma'am!" The two shared a good laugh as Joshua slowed the car back to a normal speed.

It seemed like they were back in Pine Ridge in no time, and soon, Joshua was turning the car down the street towards Sheila's house. He was a little dismayed to see some of Sheila's friends hanging around the front of the house. He glanced over to look at Sheila and saw she had a very grim look on her face. She didn't say a word to him as she opened the car door the instant the car stopped moving and got out. He got out of the car as quickly as he could, but she was already halfway to the group that was waiting for her.

"Hey, baby, it's about time you got back. Get rid of that preacher-boy, so you can come run with your own kind again. We're getting ready to party hard tonight!"

The boy speaking was dressed like something out of a horror movie and Joshua didn't like the way he was looking at Sheila. Worse still, Sheila was smiling seductively and walking towards him like she was happy to see him again, with her arms outstretched. After all they'd been through and how Sheila had changed, he was in shock seeing her appear to go right back to the person she was before they left. As she got closer, the boy stretched out his arms too, to embrace her.

"It's good to see you, again, babe, let's get away from preacher-boy and go do our thing."

The boy didn't see what was coming next at all. Neither did Joshua. Just as Sheila's arms embraced him, her right knee came up into his crotch as forcefully as she could drive it. The boy immediately crumpled to the ground in pain and moaning. As he rolled over on his back, Sheila stepped forward and placed her foot on his throat and it appeared she was putting quite a bit of weight on it.

"Listen up. Preacher-boy, there, is ten times the man you'll ever be. You'd be wise to take a page from his book and learn something. As for getting away, that's something you should be doing as soon as I let you up. If I ever see you around here again, you're going to get even worse the next time, understand?"

The boy nodded weakly and moaned. His friends looked at Sheila with shock and disbelief. Sheila lifted her foot from his throat and stepped away. Two of his friends immediately rushed over to help the boy to his feet and they all started to move back towards their cars to leave.

Sheila looked back to Joshua, who was standing there with his mouth wide open, hardly believing what he had just seen.

"C'mon, preacher-boy, we have a job to do." Sheila winked at Joshua as she called him preacher-boy.

As soon as they stepped inside the door, Sheila called out, "mom! I'm home!"

Her mother appeared, a puzzled look was on her face as Sheila usually was not one to announce herself. Her puzzled look became one of complete shock when Sheila gave her a big hug.

"Oh, mama, I'm so very sorry for the way I've acted and anything I've ever done to hurt you. Please forgive me."

Mrs. Friede was so shocked she had to sit down.

"Excuse us, mom, Joshua and I have something to take care of, but we'll sit down and talk more later, okay?"

Mrs. Friede nodded quietly, still in shock and barely believing this suddenly polite person was really her daughter.

"Let's go, Joshua!"

Sheila didn't give Joshua a chance to reply as she ran up the stairs to Sarah's room as fast as she could. By the time Joshua had caught up, Sheila was already sitting on the bed talking to Sarah.

"Forgive me sis. I haven't been a good sister at all. But...I have a surprise for you. Thanks to Joshua, I've gotten to know Jesus. Now we're sisters in more ways than one!

Sarah smiled, but the disease left her too weak to speak.

"We have another surprise, too. Joshua, do you have the stuff out of your backpack yet?"

Joshua reached into his backpack, pulled out the bottle of tea Adriel had sent with them, and handed it to Sheila.

"Her you go, sis," Sheila said as she helped Sarah slowly drink the tea. "This should fix you right up."

Sarah's eyes grew wide and she spoke softly. "What is this stuff? I can feel a difference already!"

"Let's just say a friend gave us the ingredients and another friend cooked it up for us. Maybe someday I'll be able to explain it to you. As for now, we'll just let you rest and recuperate. I've got some things to take care of."

Sarah nodded quietly, a large smile filling her face. Sheila closed the door quietly as she and Joshua stepped out into the hall.

"Looks like everything's going to work out fine, thanks to God...and you."

"I have to give God the glory..." Sheila touched a finger to his lips to silence him.

"We both know what God did for us. Now it's time for

me to set things right with mom. I can't thank you enough for everything. I hate to kick you out, but I'm going to walk you to your car so I can start turning into the daughter and sister I need to be here."

Joshua nodded, understanding Sheila wanted to rebuild her ties with her family. The two of them walked silently down the steps, past the still in shock Mrs. Friede, and out the front door back to Joshua's car.

"Joshua, I took the liberty of grabbing your cell number. Is it okay if I call you so we could maybe hang out some and you could teach me more about Jesus?"

"Sure, I'd like that."

Sheila leaned over and gave Joshua a kiss on the cheek. "I'll like it too. And I'd like to meet your dad and father both. I think I have a lot I can learn from all of you."

"Knowing them the way I do, they'll be nothing less than overjoyed to help you out. It's a little crazy when we're all together, but I think you'll fit in."

"So do I, Joshua. So do I."

As Joshua drove away, watching Sheila waving in his rearview mirror, he had a feeling there were more adventures ahead.

ABOUT THE AUTHOR

The author was born, raised, and has spent his entire life, living in Pennsylvania where each day contains the magnificent marvels of God's creation all around.

If you like this story, or the character of Joshua Carson, please read the other novels by D.L. Ford and learn the backstory behind this one.

"The Jesus Rock"
"The Trials of Jim Dunning"